WANTON WAGER

A WHITECHAPEL WAGERS NOVELLA

CHRISTY CARLYLE

Scandalous Wager

Copyright: Christy Carlyle
Published: June 2014
Cover Design: Gilded Heart Design

CHAPTER 1

He has a terrible predilection for death.

The thought dominated Captain William Selsby's mind as he sat in the study of Frederick, Lord Ashdowne, drank the man's brandy, and studied the collection of stuffed fowl, fox, deer, and boars' heads decorating every wall and flat surface. The creatures stared back at Will with glass eyes and what he imagined was a glare of resentment for the state he found them in.

He had just whipped the aristocrat quite neatly at a game of cards and would have been content to collect his winnings and be on his way, but Ashdowne had cajoled him into stopping for a bit of libation and another round of cards.

"Your hand is shaking, old man. Sure you're up for another game?"

Flexing his left hand, Will attempted to ease the spike of pain that shot down his arm. Eight years had done nothing to eradicate the ache, though he had grown used to it, learned how to accommodate it. If nothing else, he had become

1

skilled at drowning it, and in liquor far less tasty than the amber fire Freddy continued to pour from a seemingly bottomless crystal decanter.

A bird, a fragile little thing in life, now even more delicate in perpetual stuffed existence, gazed at him with a single black bead eye from the table at his side. His thoughts wandered to a memories of another eye—the wild, terrified gaze of his war horse, Hercules, as they lay together, both wounded, with Will's broken leg caught beneath the stallion's massive body. The ache in his leg began to thrum, as if his body's memory of the injury was as keen as his mind's.

A decade earlier a display of preserved animals would have escaped his notice. As a medical student he had been more interested in human anatomy and physiology rather than that of animals. But most of all he had been brash and foolish, as heedless of death as he was careless with his life. He had been eager to join the army and even hungrier for battle. Nowadays he wished he could stumble upon his younger self in a back alley and clip the arrogant blighter on the chin. What a fool he had been. What a fool he had become.

Will lifted a snifter to his lips and tipped more brandy into his mouth. He savored the burn lancing down his throat, into his chest, the heat swelling out to give him a brief sense of warmth and comfort.

"Marvelous specimens, are they not, Selsby?"

Will bit his tongue to still his honest retort and formed a more diplomatic response. "I have never seen such an extensive collection."

"They are all the work of my own hand, you know. Killed them myself. Skinned them myself. Stuffed them myself. The old bear detests my hobby. Only makes me more keen."

Ashdowne had a ferocious grin, giving the impression he

had just finished some particularly nasty business and was quite proud of himself. Will knew the man well enough to know "the old bear" referred to Freddy's father. Something to do with the family's coat of arms which featured a black bear—up on two legs, claws at the ready, and as ferocious as Freddy's grin. Though he had never explained it to Will, Ashdowne's hatred for his father was palpable. It was likely something to do with Freddy's impatience. When the earl shuffled off his mortal coil, Ashdowne, his first born son, would inherit all the old man's lands and titles.

"Quite a talent." It was the only response Will could muster, and it wasn't a lie. Freddy had a definite skill for taxidermy, and Will thought it worth pointing out, since he had never found much else to admire about the man. Spending time with Ashdowne, which he usually only did at the gentleman's club where they had met, always made Will ill at ease, as if an invisible current of energy he could not itch was crawling across his skin.

Freddy flashed him one of his savage grins, managing to look more self-satisfied than usual, and stood to approach the fireplace. He lifted a polished brass poker and tormented the coals in the grate for a bit, stoking bright flames into life.

"I did not invite you here to speak of my collection, old man. Nor to best me at cards."

Now they were coming to the point. Finally. Will had only accepted the man's invitation to his Grosvenor Square townhouse to satisfy Kate, his sister, who spent far too much time urging him to get out into society, to visit with friends, to live again.

"I have a proposition for you, Selsby. One that I believe will do you a great deal of good and will relieve me of a rather embarrassing problem."

Will was intrigued despite every instinct he had about

Lord Ashdowne. Meeting the man's gaze, Will lifted an eyebrow, urging him to go on.

Ashdowne grinned, more knowing than fierce, and settled himself in the wingback chair adjacent to the fire and across from Will. He took time arranging his limbs, crossing his long, slim legs and smoothing his palms over the intricately woven antimacassars on the chair's arms.

"When is the last time you had a woman, Selsby?"

Will choked on the swig a brandy and lifted a hand to his mouth as he coughed and swiped the potent liquid from his lips. His voice was husky when he could find the breath to reply.

"That's out of order, Ashdowne. None of your damned business and certainly none of your concern."

"Mmm. That long, is it?"

It wasn't worth it. Whatever money he might win from besting Ashdowne at cards, it was not worth being subjected to the man's salacious assumptions, nor his pity. And it was the pity that stung most intensely. He had read it in so many gazes in the last eight years, and he still saw it there in his sister's eyes nearly every day. He had left Afghanistan with a shattered leg, but it had not affected his ability as a man. The enemy had attempted to cut off his arm, not his manhood.

The truth stung too. The truth was he had been without a woman for the past eight years. When he'd returned from the war and learned that Emilia had married during his absence, he had longed—for just a moment—for death. He had wished to join Hercules in whatever existence or nothingness lay beyond the veil of life. Hercules should have been spared. God knew the beast would have gone on to be useful, valiant and ever brave.

Will closed his eyes and released a sigh so deep it burned his chest. "It has been that long."

"Then my proposition is fortuitous. As you may have heard, I am betrothed to Miss Bramson."

Will had heard of Ashdowne's betrothal. Kate took an uncharacteristic interest in aristocratic tittle tattle and was a devoted reader of several scandal rags. She even claimed to have met the Bramson woman at some lady's society meeting.

"I am aware. Please accept my belated congratulations."

Freddy literally waved off his well wishes, raising his hand in a dismissive gesture.

"Yes, well, my impending marriage lends urgency to my proposal. There is a woman in Whitechapel—"

"Tell me you don't still go sporting in Whitechapel. Surely you have outgrown such nonsense. Especially now, with a madman on the loose."

Kate's newspapers carried nearly daily stories regarding the horrific attacks on several women in the East End district. The details were so disturbing she would set the papers aside, but she always returned to read them, sometimes recounting bits to Will aloud, her voice tinged with sadness and a thread of fear.

"Worry not, old man. My sporting days are over, but there is a single matter I must tie up."

Sporting was what the young men of the club called it when a group ventured into Whitechapel or another East End district to drink, gamble, carouse, and pursue every sin available for a handful of coins. Will had joined in only once and woken the next day in an opium den in Limehouse with no memory of how he'd got there, barely a memory of his own name. The experience, the loss of control, had soured him on ever attempting such a venture again.

Frederick was still talking, though Will missed some of what he'd said.

"So you see I must find some way to distance myself from

her. She's quite lovely. I am sure you would find her desirable. She does not ask for much, and I—"

"You're offering me your whore?"

"That is a distasteful word."

"This is a distasteful business."

"You won't say that once you've tasted her."

The man was loathsome. Will stood to leave, the stiffness in his leg slowing his progress and creaking in protest. He grasped his cane and leaned on it more heavily than he liked.

"Forget my winnings from our first round and this wager of yours, Ashdowne. Keep your money and your…mistress."

"You far too honorable fool. She is a young woman who has given me a good deal of comfort over the past year. She could do the same for you."

Will turned and tried to take a step toward the door of Ashdowne's study but realized his leg had gone numb while he sat. He waited until the sensation of pins stuck in his flesh began to ease.

"I shudder to think what will happen to her once I discard her. She will become one of those creatures that murderer hunts."

Will tipped his head back and closed his eyes. Flashes of the illustrations from Kate's newspapers whirled in his mind. He could not imagine the kind of poverty that would force a woman to sell her body so she might earn doss money for one night's shelter.

Could he protect this young woman from the same fate? Yet what kind of a monster would he be to expect her to lay with him for such protection?

"Give the woman enough money to keep herself from an ugly future, Ashdowne. You must have enough to spare."

Ashdowne laughed, but it wasn't his usual deep chortle. It was brittle and sharp, souring his already high voice. "You know nothing, Selsby. I barely have enough ready cash to pay your winnings this night. Do you have any notion what it costs to maintain this residence, an estate in Derbyshire, and my ridiculous sisters?"

Will glanced back at the man and realized Ashdowne was not only distasteful but pitiable. Yet Ashdowne seemed to have no notion of how he appeared to Will. He still stood tall and proud, wearing a self-assured smirk on his narrow mouth.

"She has red hair, Selsby. Just like your Emilia."

The air left Will's lungs as if Freddy had punched him. He ducked his head and took a deep breath.

He could not recall if Ashdowne had ever met Emilia. Will did not think so, and yet the gleam in Ashdowne's eyes told Will the man knew he had found his mark. Emilia had red hair, and she was the only woman Will had ever cared for, ever considered marrying. She had rather famously broken their engagement to marry a duke, one of the most impressive catches of the season that year. The year he had returned wounded and broken from Afghanistan.

And now there was a red-haired woman in Whitechapel, a woman who was about to lose her protector, her security. The soldier in Will wanted to protect her, the man in him wanted to meet her, to see the loveliness that Ashdowne touted. And though he would never admit it to the man smiling at him wolfishly from across the room, Will harbored a sliver of hope that she might offer him what she had given to Freddy. Comfort, he had said. Will would give anything, everything, for one moment of a woman's comfort.

"Shall we play for her? Forget the winnings you stacked up earlier. One last round and winner takes all." The man had no scruples whatsoever.

"You have already said you wish to be rid of her. It is hardly a wager."

"If you win, I shall relinquish her to you completely. If I

win, I will treat myself to one more moment in her arms. Then I shall tell you her name and where to find her."

The thought of Ashdowne touching this woman again, whoever she was, made Will's stomach turn. He had enjoyed beating Ashdowne in their first round, but this time it wasn't about besting him. It was about doing anything he could to prevent the man from winning.

CHAPTER 2

"WATCH YERSELF, MISSUS!"

Ada Hamilton's eyes snapped open. She had collided with a man in a filthy woolen coat, and his shout and the pungent smell of his clothing roused her from a kind of waking sleep. She blinked, startled and frightened to find herself in the man's arms, and pushed away from him. He flashed a toothless grin and held her arm to steady her before letting go.

Though daylight had fled long ago, the Whitechapel Road was as crowded and noisy as earlier in the day. The costermongers were gone now or perhaps they were part of the throng who spent a long day working and now turned their attention to other business—finding a pint, a companion, and a place to sleep for the night.

Ada paid them no mind. A few more steps and she would be at her door, but her legs were sore and she battled to keep her eyes open. She could not recall a more wearying day. Every inch of her body ached, and her feet, confined in tightly laced boots, protested most of all. The charity hospital where she worked as a probationary nurse had been overflowing with the sick, wounded, and dying, more than they usually saw in an entire week. And after her shift she had gone door to door among their neighbors and inquired if any of them had seen or heard anything of her sister, Beth. Some wished to help, others wished her gone, but none had provided a shred of information about the girl's whereabouts. With the ominous thunderclouds hanging overhead, it was easy to fancy that God was displeased with Whitechapel and everyone in it, as one doctor had mused during the long, tiring day.

"Pardon me, sir." She had already passed the man she unknowingly plowed into, but her exhausted mind remembered too late that she should offer some apology for her misstep. He wouldn't hear her through the fog, but guilt demanded she atone for her carelessness. Then she caught sight of the pub's glowing windows and nothing else mattered beyond getting inside.

Warm light spilled out of The Golden Bell, and the scent of pipe smoke, roasted sausages, and stale beer beckoned. Ada did not trust her tired legs to make it up the side stairs that led directly to her family's living quarters. Instead, she stumbled straight through the doors of the pub like any other patron desperate for grog.

As the door closed behind her, she was enveloped in heat and sound. The fireplace was roaring on the stormy November night, and the pub was filled to the rafters with men and women who must have wished to escape the chill as much as Ada did.

She scanned the bar for any sight of her mother but only glimpsed the bulky figure of Harry, their giant of a barman, who ruled The Golden Bell with a ready smile and an iron fist. When Harry was about there was very little mischief from their patrons, no matter how much liquor they consumed.

Ada raised a hand to wave at him, the motion requiring much more effort than expected, and caught his eye. His grin fled as he left his station behind the bar and pushed his way through the crowded pub. It seemed only a moment later he was by her side, a massive arm around her shoulders, escorting her toward the wooden door at the end of the bar.

"Go on up to your mum, miss. She is that anxious to speak with you."

Ada stopped and looked up at him. "Is there news of Beth?"

Harry shook his head and his broad shoulders seemed to sag. "No, miss. Not a word. But Mrs. 'Amilton is anxious, int she?"

Always. Mama was always anxious. Ada could not remember a time when her mother was not nervous, worried, or at her wits end. As the eldest of three surviving siblings, Ada spent much of her childhood fearing she was the cause of Mama's hand wringing. But Father had caused his share of misery too, drinking the pub's stock and frittering away its profits before he disappeared.

There were rumors he had been in a fight in Limehouse, a brawl over a card game. Some said he had died there on the pier and been discarded in the Thames. They looked for him for months before Mama found a crumpled note inside a drawer. In it, George Hamilton made a half-hearted attempt to explain why he was not suited to marriage or fatherhood. Mama thought he would return one day. Ada knew they must go on, father or no father. There was a pub to run, and Beth and Vicky needed stability, if such a thing was possible with Mama's constant fussing.

But now there was reason to fuss. Beth had "gone astray," as Mama put it. Ada thought her claims of catching an earl another of the girl's fanciful boasts, but now her sister was nowhere to be found. It had been four days and no one had heard from or seen her.

"I'll go up. Thank you, Harry. Will you be all right closing up on your own?"

He shot her a look indicating her question was foolish. Though her parents owned the The Golden Bell, Harry was defacto steward and manager, overseeing every aspect of running the busy pub. He had been a godsend when her father hired him years before. It was her father's one legacy that Ada could be grateful for, that and his insistence she and all his children go to school and obtain a decent education.

"Thank you." Ada spoke the word around an unladylike yawn and pressed a hand to her mouth to stifle it.

"Seems you're in need of a good kip."

"There has been little of that since Beth went..." Ada could not finish the thought. Her sister was missing. No one had seen her in over a week, yet to voice the words gave the fact permanence, a certainty she still wished to deny. She could not bring herself to read the papers and see details of the unsolved murders of women who lived and worked just streets away from their home. But that wouldn't be Beth's fate. They struggled, but there had never been a need for the girl to sell her body for food or a place to rest her head. It was more likely the silly little creature had gone off with this man she boasted about day and night. Pray God they went all the way to Gretna Green and Beth might come back a respectable woman. Ada had been trying for days to learn more about the man Beth had referred to in the days before she vanished.

"Aye, miss Ada. We'll find the lass. Go see to the missus. Leave the rest to me."

· · ·

"IF ONLY YOUR FATHER WERE HERE." Her mother stood ringing a wet rag between her hands as she repeated her daily lament. Ada allowed her mother to moan but knew her father's presence would do nothing to alleviate the problems of running their pub or solve the mystery of Beth's disappearance.

Though he hadn't helped much when he'd been alive, she imagined her father must have been an industrious man at some stage of his life. He had decided to purchase the pub, after all, and Mother said Whitechapel had been different then.

"'Nother ale here, man. 'As the well run dry?" Angus McCutcheon's wail came straight up from the pub through the floorboards of their upstairs living quarters and rattled Ada's nerves. His cry was so vehement it made her mother jump. Ada couldn't bear to see the fear and distress in her mother's eyes.

"I will speak to him, Mother."

"No, girl. Don't say it. Harry is much better suited to such trouble."

It was undoubtedly true, but leaving everything to one man and the skeleton crew who assisted him didn't seem fair. Though Ada had no interest in managing the pub, she wished her mother would make more of an effort. At two and forty, she was still young, and if she were half as industrious as she was fretful, Ada thought they might all be happier.

"Very well. I shall leave it to Harry. Especially tonight. I am dead on my feet."

Ada's mother looked up at her through damp lashes and spoke in a voice she could barely make out, but she did not need to hear the words clearly. It was a question her mother had asked every night for the past four nights.

"Any word of Beth?"

Ada could not look her in the eye. There was no word of

Beth, hadn't been since the Monday before. Ada had knocked on doors, sent notes along to a few family members who lived nearby, questioned their usual patrons at the pub—all to no avail. Beth had gone to visit Nancy, who lived just along the Whitechapel Road. Nancy did piecework sewing and Beth sometimes helped her for a few pence or as much as a shilling if it was a fancy job. Ada had always been awed at the delicate beauty Beth could render with fabric and thread. The girl had a real talent. But she was of the age when every man turned her head. This earl, if he truly existed, had certainly done so.

"Tomorrow I will go and speak with Nancy again. Beth may have sworn her to secrecy about some foolish plan, but I will make her tell me the truth. And I will go back to the station on Leman Street."

Though her mother insisted they would be no help, Ada went to the police the moment they realized Beth had not returned to her bed on Monday night. The young man at the station dutifully took down all the details Ada provided, scant as they were, and a constable called the following day— to the consternation of some of their rowdier patrons—to discover if Beth had returned home. When they told him she had not, he assured them the police would continue to make inquiries. Still, Ada had made plenty of her own.

Her mother's expression indicated her complete lack of faith in the Metropolitan Police force.

"They cannot even catch the creature slashing women all around us. How can they find one slip of a girl?"

It was no use arguing with her. The only thing that seemed useful was a few hours of sleep.

"Get some sleep, Mother. We shall start again tomorrow."

Ada watched her mother walk toward her bedroom and took a moment to peek in on Vicky, who lay snug in her cot cuddling a ragged stuffed bear, before cleaning up in the wash basin and lowering herself onto her own narrow bed.

Sleep swept down on her swiftly and she let herself sink into it. It was still early evening, though it had been one of the longest days she could ever remember. The pub still reverberated with conversation, the clink of dishes, and the occasional angry shout, courtesy of toughs like Angus McCutcheon. But the sounds were familiar to Ada, comforting. She turned her head on the pillow and knew she would finally sleep.

"Miss Ada."

A hand lay heavy on her shoulder and her first thought was to push it away. Sleep was a sweet balm, a deep, dark abyss she did not want to come out of. But her arms were pinned beneath the blanket and she came more fully awake.

One thought consumed her. Beth.

She bolted up and recognized Billy in the dim light of the room. As assistant to Harry, part-time barman, and occasional help to the cook, he must have been the obvious man to spare to come and wake her.

"Is it Beth?"

"No, miss. It's a gentleman 'ere to see you."

"A gentleman? Who?"

"Never saw 'im before in me life. I was of a mind to send the toff on his way, but then I thought. Well, maybe 'e knows sumfink of your sister."

"Did he ask for me directly?"

Billy shook his head. "Just asked for Miss 'Amilton."

Could it be this Frederick gentleman Beth had spoken of? If it was, would he have answers about Beth's whereabouts? Ada couldn't stifle the hope bubbling up inside.

CHAPTER 3

WILL DID NOT EXPECT TO FIND MISS HAMILTON LIVING ABOVE a taproom in Whitechapel. He directed the hansom driver to the address Ashdowne gave him and was surprised to be dropped at the doorstep of a rather noisy, ramshackle public house. He knew he looked a fool to all those who spared him a glance, dressed in his best clothes and bearing gifts for a lady. The barkeep turned out to be the least welcoming Will had ever met in his life. When Will asked for Miss Hamilton, the giant of a man turned an alarming shade of red before begrudgingly pointing to a dark stairwell near the bar.

Now, waiting in a modest yet homey room that looked to serve as the family's living area, dining area, and makeshift kitchen, Will fought the urge to leave, to seek another hansom and return to his lonely, eventless life. To forget about this business of Ashdowne's kept woman and the crime-ridden East End district where she lived.

What would he say to her? What could he say? He had been sent by her lover to see if he might be her next? The whole business was dishonorable, and yet he could not resist the desire to at least meet her. To see the red-haired beauty who gave men comfort. A shiver ran down his spine at the thought, and his leg and arm began a slow burning ache. Perhaps they had already been aching. He had learned not to notice and usually ignored his body, trying to drone out sensation. But thoughts of Miss Hamilton brought nothing but sensation.

And then she walked into the room.

Ashdowne had said her hair was red, but it was nothing like the tame amber shade of Emilia's hair. Miss Hamilton's hair was fiery, a most striking shade of true, rich red. It swept down over her shoulders in jumbled waves, and the sheen in her blue eyes and bee-stung plumpness of her full mouth suggested he'd woken her.

He was a cad, an utter wretch for disturbing this woman and expecting anything at all from her.

"Frederick?"

Could she not see clearly he was not Ashdowne? They might both be wanton wretches, but their outward appearance was not similar at all. Ashdowne was dark, with black hair and nearly black eyes. Will knew everything about his own looks was light, from his blonde-brown hair to his grey eyes.

"No, Miss Hamilton. I'm sorry. As you can see, I am not Frederick. My name is William Selsby."

Disappointment was plain on the woman's lovely face, and Will wished he'd taken that cab back to his lodgings on Moreton Terrace after all.

She rubbed her finger across the arch of her eyebrow and closed her eyes for the briefest of moments before speaking. "Forgive me, Mr. Selsby. I do not wish to be rude, but it is quite late, and I do not believe we are acquainted."

"No." How to begin? How to explain the reason he had burst into her life?

When he made no further reply, they stood and stared at

each other for a moment. Will savored the opportunity to study her. He had never seen a young woman stand so stock straight and confident. No debutante he had ever met could manage such a feat. The diminutive woman before him would put many of his own soldiers to shame.

But her stance and air of self-possession was a striking contrast to her delicate beauty—wide, full lips and strikingly beautiful blue-green eyes together with her small frame and lush curves made her seem more a manifestation from a fairy story than a flesh and blood woman he had roused from her bed in a cramped room in Whitechapel.

She let out a sigh. "Then why are you here, Mr. Selsby? What business could you have with me at this hour?"

She studied him then, skimming her gaze down his body in an assessing manner that made his skin burn beneath his evening wear. She focused her gaze on the items in his hands. Ashdowne had advised him to bring flowers and a small gift to encourage amity with Miss Hamilton.

"You come bearing gifts, sir. Who do you expect to woo?"

Every irrational urge inside of him wanted to woo her, this petite woman with such exotic beauty and the backbone of a soldier. But the look in her eyes, the slight grimace on her face when she looked his way, told him she had no interest in furthering their acquaintance.

"Miss Hamilton, forgive me for intruding on your evening. I was directed here by Lord Ashdowne."

No flicker of recognition registered on her face. She simply continued to stare at him as if waiting for more. His explanation thus far meant nothing to her. The name Lord Ashdowne meant nothing to her.

"The man you spoke of earlier. Frederick. That is the Lord Ashdowne to whom I refer."

The moment the words were out of his mouth, Miss Hamilton launched herself across the room, closing the space between them. She touched him, grasping the lapels of his cloak, her skirts pressing into his legs, the length of her body nearly touching his. She would have crushed the roses he carried, but he lifted his arm to salvage them.

Will fought the urge to drop the silly roses and the small box containing an opal broach he'd spent far too much time selecting years ago and never given to the woman he had hoped to marry. Now he wanted his hands free to touch Miss Hamilton, to wrap an arm around her waist, to touch the red waves that tumbled over her shoulders. But she had not approached him out of desire. There was a kind of frantic desperation in her eyes.

"You know this man, this Frederick?"

They stood so close the heat of her breath feathered across his face when she spoke. They were so close Will was tempted to dip his head and take her lips in one swift movement.

"Yes, we are acquainted."

"And he sent you here? To speak with whom? With me, or with my sister?"

"Your sister?" The mention of her sister sparked brightness in her eyes, and Will realized Miss Hamilton was on the verge of tears. A surge of desire to comfort her overwhelmed him.

"Yes, my sister. Elizabeth. We call her Beth. I am Ada Hamilton. If you know anything of my sister, please tell me."

After she spoke Miss Hamilton looked down where she gripped his clothing so fiercely her hands had turned white. She seemed to realize what she had done and released his cloak, leaving the material twisted and creased, and took a step away from him.

Will missed the warmth of her, the scent of her.

"Forgive me, Mr. Selsby."

He wanted to help her but had no idea how he might. It

seemed he wasn't even sure who he had been sent to call upon. He reached into his vest pocket to retrieve the note on which Ashdowne had scribbled Miss Hamilton's address. He was certain the man had included no Christian name.

"I'm afraid Lord Ashdowne only gave me your address."

She approached him again, reaching out for the card he'd produced.

He recalled the rest of what Ashdowne had written there and pulled the paper back, but the fearsome little woman would have none of it. When he pulled back, she came closer, so close he would have given her anything she asked.

As his gaze locked with hers, she yanked the cream-colored note from his fingers. She turned toward the light cast by an oil lamp but did not move away from him. Her crimson hair was even lovelier up close with sparks of light catching a strand here and there.

He knew she would move away from him when she read what Ashdowne had written. She would know he was craven and immoral, that none of his reasons for coming here this night were the right ones.

She read, her voice breathy and deep. "With my compliments, Selsby. Be good to my Beth and she will be very good to you."

She shifted her gaze back toward him, taking in the small black box bulging in his pocket and the now drooping roses he clutched in his hand.

"My God, he gave her to you. Like some bit of property he had tired of." Her words, the tone of her voice, dripped with loathing. And when she looked at him, her extraordinary green-blue eyes were narrowed in disgust. Disgust and something more. Fury? Fear? He could not be sure. "So you came here to claim your gift from this noble lord?"

He did touch her then. He reached out. She was so close.

He touched her arm, to mediate his plea, to beg her not to loathe him. She pulled away as if he'd burned her and took three quick steps to the opposite corner of the room.

"I came for all the wrong reasons, Miss Hamilton. I do not know you. I have no right to your sister." The words dried up in his mouth and choked him with a bitter flavor, as if he'd stuffed a handful of newspaper down his throat.

He could not tell her the truth of why he had agreed to Ashdowne's cruel wager, why he had not touched a woman in nearly eight years, or why he believed the only female comfort he deserved was the kind bought with flowers and gifts and coin.

"You came here expecting to find some dollymop."

Will was shocked to hear the crude term coming out of Miss Hamilton's mouth.

He wanted to tell her he had merely come for comfort, for a moment in the company of a woman who did not look at him with pity or disgust for his frailty. The irony was that Miss Hamilton stared at him with all the disgust her beautiful countenance could muster, yet for reasons which had nothing to do with his scarred body and battered soul.

He knew what he had to do, knew what he must do, yet he was surprised to acknowledge that he did not wish to. He had to walk out of her life, to disappear so that she might forget he had ever imposed on her and assumed such horrible things about her sister.

"Forgive me, Miss Hamilton. There is nothing I can say to excuse my intrusion here. The best I can do is to leave you in peace."

Will took one last look at the woman, drinking in her unique beauty and air of poise that seemed undiminished despite the circumstances of their encounter. Then he pivoted on his boot heel and started toward the door of the small room.

"She is only eighteen."

Miss Hamilton was near tears now. Will could hear it in the shaky quality of her voice.

"He told her he wished to marry her. She never told me that, but she said it to our mother. My sister isn't a whore, Mr. Selsby. She is an impressionable girl."

Will did not know what to say. He only knew what he ached to do. He wished he could have met Miss Hamilton under any other circumstances. He wished to comfort her tears away. Most of all, he wished her sister had never encountered a cad like Freddy.

He angled his head to look at her, but she had turned her back on him.

Abandoning her stiff posture, she stood gripping the frame of a straight-backed chair as if it might support her in her misery.

"I am sorry, Miss Hamilton. I offer my sincerest apology to you and your sister, for calling here tonight, and for the damage Lord Ashdowne has done."

For several moments she said nothing, just bent slightly over the chair and wept quietly. He would not know she was sobbing except for the movement of her slim shoulders and the crushing sound of an occasional whimper.

That was it. He could not stand and watch the woman weep alone. He took a step toward her, but she lifted her pale hand, palm up, to stop him.

"Please go, Mr. Selsby. My family and I do not require your pity."

CHAPTER 4

THOUGH SHE HAD ASKED HIM TO LEAVE, THE SOUND OF MR. Selsby's retreating footsteps made Ada cry harder, to weep openly and not worry about how unladylike or weak she might appear. There was no longer any doubt about the nature of Beth's relationship with this Lord Ashdowne. It was a relationship that had gone so far as to allow the man to believe he owned Beth and had the right to hand her off to another man. The thought caused bile to rise in Ada's throat. She closed her eyes and prayed for calm.

But when she closed her eyes all she saw were the haunting grey eyes of Mr. Selsby staring back at her. She feared she might never forget his eyes. They had struck her immediately, before she knew who he was and the awful truth of why he had sought her out.

She knew the moment she walked into the room and glimpsed him in all his finery that he was not this Frederick of whom Beth had spoken. She hoped he was the man. If he had been, he might have finally provided some answers about her sister. But she had known he was not. Mr. Selby was something altogether different than a heartless aristocrat who seduced impoverished young women.

Yet, ironically, he had come for the very same purpose.

Her insides twisted and sickness nearly overwhelmed her the moment she realized the true reason for his late night visit. The perfect hothouse roses and beribboned gift box should have given her a clue. How was it possible a man with such sad, beautiful eyes could be so desperate as to use another man to procure a woman? His fine looks, bearing, and obvious wealth as displayed by his clothing would have made him a fine catch for any woman.

Why was it so difficult to feel the same disgust for William Selsby that she bore for Ashdowne?

It was the pain. Beyond the blue-flecked grey eyes, she had glimpsed a man in pain. She had seen it in so many people at the hospital. Not just physical pain, but need, the longing for human tenderness, for comfort to quell a wound that went deeper than cuts and aches and bruises.

Though he appeared outwardly fit, with his tall, lean body and bright eyes, Mr. William Selsby had been wounded. She detected a slight limp in his gait and realized his cane, as many gentleman carried, was for more than just affectation. Once she caught him wincing as he watched her. Some injury must trouble him a great deal. Yet she imagined the pain she saw in his eyes was not just about whatever accident or encounter had left his body damaged. His eyes spoke volumes more.

No one had ever looked at her as he had looked at her. Though Ada was not unaware of the gazes occasionally directed her way, she imagined most people stared at the oddity of her flame red hair. And there was one young doctor at the charity hospital who smiled at her a bit too long whenever their eyes met in the course of a busy day. But he did not look at her, did not caress her with his gaze, the way that Mr. William Selsby had. She had seen appreciation in Selsby's gaze, as if he found her pleasant to look upon, but there was something more—a heat, a sizzling burn of desire that seemed to emanate from him. He wore an expression that said he wanted her more than anything in the world. That she, above all other women, was worth having. His desire had tugged at her from across the room, curled about her body, and warmed her in places no man had ever ignited before.

But Mr. Selsby was not the man who should be kindling her senses. He was no better than the wretched aristocrat who had sent him. And that was the man she needed to speak to. Never mind the golden-haired man with warm eyes and a beautifully-shaped mouth. She needed to focus her thoughts on Frederick, Lord Ashdowne. He had to know something of Beth, where she might be, why she had gone missing. Ada shook away the idea he might be responsible for her sister's disappearance, that he might have done something unspeakable to her—like the monster who prowled the streets of Whitechapel.

A thought struck her and she took the eight steps between the upstairs and main area of the pub as quickly as she could. Most of the patrons had dispersed for the evening, and only a few weary souls still slumped against the bar or huddled at one of the corner tables.

She scanned the room for Mr. Selsby. As tall as he was, she would have been able to spy his black evening wear easily, no matter how crowded the pub. Then she saw the roses. They lay on a table not far from the bar. Wilted, they seemed to melt against the table top. She approached the empty table and stroked her finger along one velvety red petal.

"Harry? Do you recall the man who sat at this table?"

"Course I do. 'E's the toff what called on you earlier in the ev'ning."

"I need to find him."

"What for?"

"He knows the lord that Beth was always going on about. Lord Ashdowne is his name. If I could speak with him, maybe…" Ada huffed a sigh of frustration. "I do not know. Perhaps he could tell me what's happened to her."

Ada lifted a finger to her mouth to bite her nail. Mama would slap her hand if she saw her. But she wasn't there to see, and it seemed to alleviate the ceaseless churning in her stomach and the ache beginning in her head.

There must be some way to find a titled lord, even without the aid of Mr. Selsby.

Harry's deep voice startled her from her racing thoughts.

"Your man took a hansom. Old Jerrold and my brother were both working the street outside this evening. I can ask. Could be one of them what took your toff into the city."

Harry said the words as if he did not wish to do the service he had offered. She beamed the most sincere smile she could muster at half eleven on the longest day she could recall to indicate her gratitude.

"Thank you, Harry. May I help you close up?"

"No, you may not. I sent you up for your kip hours ago and 'ere you are back again."

Harry didn't say another word, just lifted the hand which held the damp rag he was using to wipe down the bar and pointed above his head, to her family's lodgings. She took his meaning and gave him a grin.

"Yes, sir, Mr. Beck. I am on my way."

Sleep was essential if she was to rise early in order to speak to Beth's friend, Nancy, again and then seek out Lord Ashdowne.

CHAPTER 5

WILL'S EYES SNAPPED OPEN AND HE WAITED FOR THE SENSE OF dread that greeted him most mornings. It was an anxiousness accompanied by hazy memories of his dreams—dreams of blood and dust, of battle cries, and the clash of steel, men, and horses. But there was no dread, only a sense of longing and the memory of a woman with quiet confidence and unusual beauty.

It was ridiculous to spare a single thought for Miss Hamilton. He would never see the woman again. Even if he wished to, she certainly had no desire to continue their association. He'd proved himself to be the worst kind of man, one ruled by his passions. Yet it was ironic she might think him a libertine when the reality was so different. If he had known passion the past handful of years, he would not have played the fool and taken Ashdowne up on his debauched wager.

He focused on the familiar ache in his arm and leg, and the thumping pain in his head. After returning from Whitechapel, the whiskey decanter had beckoned, but he could not fool himself into justifying it as medicinal. He had not been in physical pain, though his conscience gnawed at him from the moment he had arrived at Miss Hamilton's doorstep until the moment he'd returned to his own.

Banging sounded at his door to match the drumbeat in his head.

"Will, are you still abed?"

His sister would have done well in the Hussars. Rising early was as much a principle with her as a habit.

Will pulled on his trousers and a fresh shirt before answering, but Kate—never one to wait for anyone—was rattling the latch on his bedroom door.

"May I enter?"

"Do I have any choice?"

Will spoke the words with well-intended sarcasm, but they also reminded him of a matter he needed to address. It was high time his sister found some worthy cause to occupy her time and talents, if not a husband who could provide her the love and attention she deserved. He was grateful Kate had been there after his return from the war, and she had been tireless at nursing him back to health. But he was back on his own two feet, and it wasn't fair to hamper his sister's second chance for marriage and a family of her own.

"No, I suppose you don't." Kate entered the room with a small tray laden with a bowl of porridge and a steaming cup of coffee. Will didn't even try to stifle his smile.

Six years his junior at nine and twenty, Kate was still a vibrant, intelligent woman with much to offer any suitor. Her widowhood at nineteen was far behind her, though Will had rarely detected any urgency or even real interest on her part to marry again. Yet it would be for the best. He could not allow his sister to be wasted on spinsterhood and caretaking for her older brother.

It suited them to lodge together at the moment, but he knew she would be happier as mistress of her own home.

"Don't even consider getting used to such treatment." She set the tray on the table near his chair by the fireplace and turned to him, her hands planted firmly on her hips. "I heard you come in late last evening. Far too late. And you woke me when you stumbled to your bed long after midnight. Dare I ask?"

Though her face was fixed in a stern expression, Will heard no real anger in his sister's tone. She worried over him to a ridiculous degree, especially considering he was the elder between them. But Kate took after their mother, a bit heavy-handed in everything she did and eager to know the whys and wherefores of everyone's business. With Kate, still quite young and lovely, most were willing to dismiss her manner as simple curiosity or a bit too much exuberance. With their mother, it was not unusual to hear even her own brother refer to her as a harridan. Will hoped Kate would not end up bearing the moniker one day.

"It was to do with Lord Ashdowne. You did wish me to renew my acquaintance with him."

"But you did not take the carriage. Don't tell me you walked all the way to Lord Ashdowne's and back in the middle of the night."

A sizable inheritance from their father meant Will could afford to keep a brougham, and he was not surprised Kate was attuned to its comings and goings.

"I took a hansom." It was the truth, the part it was easy to tell, even if he could not bring himself to admit the rest.

"Why on earth would you take a hansom when you have a perfectly good carriage at your disposal?"

"Whimsy?"

She glowered at him now. It was another trait she had inherited from their mother, though Will admitted Kate had perfected the art.

"I am going to call on Ashdowne this afternoon as well. I

shall take the carriage this time if it puts you at ease." He knew she did not give a fig how he traveled, though she may have worried how his leg would hold out for the handful of miles between Ashdowne's Mayfair townhouse and theirs in the slightly less fashionable part of the London. "There is an unresolved matter between us."

Will took a sip of his coffee, now more warm than hot but still strong and satisfying, and avoided his sister's direct gaze.

"That sounds ominous." She had abandoned her school mistress stance and began tidying his room as she spoke.

"Kate, leave it. I can look after myself. And what I cannot tidy, Sally will see to." Their single housemaid was affable and reliable, but her sense of clean and his sister's were ever at odds. "And there is nothing ominous regarding my business with Ashdowne."

It was as close to lying to his sister as Will had ever come.

"Then what must you see him about?" She wanted details. And the less he was willing to divulge, the more she would dig.

"Just the matter of a wager."

She heaved a sigh as if his revelation was an enormous letdown.

"Oh, you gentlemen and your wagers."

Were they gentlemen? Little did she know how far he and Ashdowne had fallen from gentlemanly wagers.

* * *

"Where are you going in such a hurry, Ada? And why have you not told Mama?"

Ada's twelve-year-old sister Vicky was born to be a sentry. She had a quick eye and even quicker mind, and Ada had never met another person with a keener memory for details. She should have known she could not dress and break her fast and leave their lodgings without Vicky taking notice.

"Mama and I spoke last evening. She knows I am going to speak with Nancy again this morning."

"About Beth?"

Vicky's voice wobbled a bit whenever she spoke Beth's name and it sent a stab of misery straight through Ada. She reassured Vicky every day, but she could not expect the child not to worry as fiercely as she did for their sister's safety.

"Yes, darling, about Beth. And there is someone else I must speak to as well. He may know something about Beth that can help us find her." As soon as Ada spoke the words, she wished she could take them back. They sounded too hopeful, even to her own ears. The last thing she wanted to do was give Vicky false hope, yet neither could she stomach lying to her.

"Is it Ashdowne?"

"How do you know that name?" Had Beth divulged more to their little sister than she had to Ada or their mother?

Vicky reached into the folds of her skirt, into the tiny pocket that Beth sewed into every one of them for her, and produced a cream-colored piece of paper. It was the piece of paper Ada had taken from Mr. Selsby, the one with their address and Lord Ashdowne's tasteless message written on one side. Ada took the card Vicky offered, flipped it over, and looked at the opposite side.

Ashdowne. Four Grosvenor Square.

"You're not cross, are you? That I took it? I was going to give it to you. I promise I was. I only just found it in the sitting room where I heard you arguing with that man last evening."

Vicky's words tumbled out on top of one another, the way they always did when she was trying to talk her way out of a scolding.

Ada reached out to clasp her sister's hands. "Vicky, calm yourself. No, I'm not cross. In fact, I am very grateful you found it. But I was not arguing with that man last evening, and you were meant to be in your bed."

The girl looked momentarily pleased with herself and then contrite. "I was asleep, but then I woke. You did raise your voice to him at least once, though his voice always remained the same. It was very pleasant, was it not?"

Vicky was right. She usually was. Ada had raised her voice to Mr. Selsby, and he did have an undeniably pleasant voice. It was a voice she had heard in her head from the moment she woke, as she went over every word between them again and again.

It was a good thing Vicky had not caught a glimpse of the man. She did not want to be reminded of how handsome he was, though she did not need reminding. She could not shake the memory of his face, and his haunted grey eyes.

"Yes, dear."

"Does that man—the one with the kind voice—know where Beth is?"

He didn't even know who Beth was, and he had come looking for her, so he could have had nothing to do with the girl's disappearance. Yet something inside of Ada yearned to speak to him of the situation with her sister. She told herself it was because he might reveal details about Ashdowne the man would not divulge himself. She tried not to think of the real reason he had come seeking her sister.

"No. I'm afraid he knows nothing about it at all." No, Mr. Selsby knew nothing, and the pain and desire she saw reflected in his gaze represented just the sort of complication she did not wish to admit into her heart and mind. His intentions had been completely dishonorable.

Now if only she could forget him.

CHAPTER 6

WILL REACHED ASHDOWNE'S FRONT DOOR EARLIER THAN THE fashionable hour for morning calls. He had to speak his piece with the man and then see what he could do about the younger Miss Hamilton. If Ashdowne would not settle some funds on her and make amends for his deception, Will would do what he could, despite whatever objections the elder Miss Hamilton might have. He suspected she would have plenty.

The same butler who answered his knock earlier in the week opened the door of Ashdowne's townhouse. The man was young and his arrogant bearing matched his master's.

"I wish to speak with Lord Ashdowne." Will could hear voices from within the house as he spoke. It seemed the Ashdownes were entertaining early, but now that he was on the man's doorstep, he wouldn't be deterred.

"Of course, Captain Selsby."

Perhaps the chap was more accommodating than he looked.

He lad lifted an arm to point toward the study where he had waited for Frederick the first time he had visited.

"May I take your coat and hat, sir? I shall inform Lord Ashdowne you have arrived for the early luncheon."

The last thing Will wanted to do was sit down at table with Ashdowne, but he did not have a chance to explain that he only wished to speak with the man for a moment. The butler ushered him into the room quickly and exited with as much haste, closing the door behind him.

Ashdowne's stuffed menagerie stared down at him as Will waited a quarter of an hour before the aristocrat entered the room, dressed in a fine suit more suited to evening wear than a morning luncheon. He looked every inch the titled lord, and he was beaming, in high spirits and wearing his signature wolfish grin.

"Selsby, didn't expect to see you again so soon, old man. Do not tell me you've come to regale me with tales of my flame-haired East End lovely. I couldn't bear it." He bent toward Will as if to impart a secret. "Truth be told, I already miss the girl. I did not exaggerate her charms, eh, Selsby?"

If Ashdowne was talking about the same woman Will met last evening, then he would have to agree. Amply endowed with many charms, Miss Hamilton could easily entice a man, but Ashdowne was referring to an eighteen-year-old young woman who believed his intentions had been honorable.

"I never met Beth. I met her sister."

"Sister? Ah yes, older, I believe. My Beth gave me to believe she was a bit of a spinster. Never met her."

The ease with which Ashdowne dismissed Ada Hamilton gave Will a surge of satisfaction. He was pleased the man had never set eyes on her and did not refer to her in the possessive way he did her sister.

"Is she a redhead too?"

Will ignored the question, though a flash of her crimson hair passed in his mind's eye. He could remember every detail of its shade, and the way the lamplight set it aglow.

"Miss Hamilton tells me you seduced her sister by promising to marry her."

Ashdowne had been busying himself with retrieving a cigarette from a silver case. At Will's words, he thrust the cigarette into the fireplace.

"That is ridiculous! I never promised the girl any such thing. It was some silly notion she dreamed up all on her own. Said she was afraid she might get with child and then were would she be. Thank the gods she never did." He took another cigarette out of the case and placed it between his lips. Without lighting or removing it, he spoke around it. "I will tell you this though, Selsby. The girl required no persuading. She was as ripe as late summer fruit."

Will caressed the head of his cane and ached with the desire to wipe the lecherous grin off of Ashdowne's face.

When he was angriest, Will strove for calm, reason raging against instinct.

Slowly and carefully he spoke each word he had come to say. "You will put this right with the girl and her family. Send them money, enough for the girl to settle into a comfortable life. Enough for the mistakes she has made not to haunt her. I do not care about your financial troubles, Ashdowne. Do something decent for this young woman you have wronged."

For a moment, Ashdowne merely stared at him as if Will had gone mad. Then he bowed his head, and Will wondered if he might be feeling a bit of shame, a sliver of repentance. He lifted his head and Will saw the smile on his face and heard the chortle bubbling up his throat. The man laughed loudly, holding his belly as if unable to contain his mirth. Then he took two steps forward, toward Will, and held his hand out as if to shake his hand.

"Congratulations, Selsby. You truly are the most honorable fool I have ever met."

But Will knew he wasn't honorable. He had gone to

Whitechapel to seek out Beth Hamilton to sate the same hunger that drove Ashdowne. In the end, he had only met her sister and now couldn't get the woman out of his mind. Oh, he was a fool, but honor had nothing to do with it.

He ignored Ashdowne's hand, though his smug face was just close enough...

"Freddy, whatever are you doing in here? Have you forgotten our guests?"

A woman with the same dark hair and eyes as Ashdowne swept into the room. She was too young to be anything other than man's sister, but Will had never met her.

"Captain Selsby. How wonderful." The woman approached him in a cloud of peach silk, and took him by the arm as if he was a long lost friend. "You are so good to have come on such short notice to even out our numbers for dinner. Dr. Tully bid off for the morning luncheon, so we were uneven. But now you will supply our deficit. It's just...wonderful."

"My God, Hetty, you have not even been properly introduced to the man."

Ashdowne seemed truly put out by his sister's social faux pas, and Will would have laughed at the man's hypocrisy if the situation was not so awkward.

"Selsby, this is my sister, Lady Harriet. Hetty, apparently you already know Captain Selsby."

"Only by reputation."

Will knew of no reputation he could claim that would make him known to an earl's daughter. When he arched a brow in her direction, she explained.

"You poor man. I know of your heroic sacrifices, Captain. You are quite the hero in my book."

Will detached the woman's fingers from his jacket sleeve as gently as he was able as he spoke. "I am nothing of the sort, Lady Harriet. I was wounded, and I survived the war. That is all."

"Oh pish posh. I know your sister, Katherine. We both do charity work at the Bethlem Orphanage. She has told me the most horrific stories of your bravery. Every time I hear the one about your horse, I am positively miserable." The woman's sharp, white smile belied her claim.

Will was surprised to hear that his sister spoke of him in heroic terms. If anything, he'd believed himself a bit of a burden to her since his return from Afghanistan.

Will offered Lady Harriet a smile he hoped looked more sincere than it felt. "You cannot expect a sister to do anything but embellish her brother's exploits."

The lady shot her brother a look over Will's shoulder. "I am not certain I agree, Captain. I have never been tempted to embellish any of my tales about Freddy. And I have plenty of them to tell."

The enmity between the siblings sparked to life like dry kindling.

"Run along, Hetty. Selsby and I will be there directly."

Will was surprised Ashdowne's sister immediately obeyed his command and left them alone. He did not have to remind Ashdowne of the reason for his visit. The man offered his answer.

"I will not give the girl a shilling, Selsby. I have paid for what I wanted, and she has benefited greatly from our... acquaintance. If you're so keen on playing hero, go and give her money yourself. Or give it to her sister, who probably has a much cleverer head on her shoulders."

"She won't take it."

"The sister. Did you already offer her money?"

"No. But after meeting with her, I am under the impression she would not look kindly on charity."

Ashdowne studied him, and Will almost looked away, eager to hide whatever Ashdowne was seeking.

"You are taken with the woman."

Ashdowne seemed to find great glee in the observation, and Will loathed how insightful it was.

"My knowledge of her consists of a brief conversation, Ashdowne. Hardly taken."

As if to prove him a liar, Will heard the voice of Miss Ada Hamilton. Her speech held a certain timbre and warmth he would recognize anywhere and for the rest of his life.

It came from the direction of the foyer. When Will turned his head toward the sound, Ashdowne seemed to notice it too. Unhampered by a cane or limp, he beat Will to the doorframe and swung the door open. Lady Harriet approached from the opposite hall, shouting in a sort of high-pitched whine.

"Who in the world is shouting in my foyer? We have guests, Collier! Quiet the woman down."

Miss Hamilton emerged from the open front door, sweeping past the young butler, and toward Lady Harriet.

"My lady, please. I must speak with Lord Ashdowne."

Miss Hamilton looked magnificent, even with her hair constrained in an artful arrangement, every bit the proper lady. Will's body charged with a kind of electric hum at the sight of her. She exuded a magnetic force that drew him.

Ashdowne seemed to guess at her identity, no doubt from the stunning shade of her hair. His smile was predatory.

"Miss Hamilton, I presume. My, my, Selsby. I see now why you were so easily smitten. She's even prettier than her sister."

At the sound of Ashdowne's voice, Miss Hamilton turned her head in his direction, but her gaze skimmed past him and she looked at Will.

"Mr. Selsby."

Her tone held a note of disappointment that lanced at Will's gut. What must she think to find him with Lord Ashdowne? His impulse was to go to her, to help her, to let her know she did not need anything from Ashdowne. Will would put things right, even if the aristocrat refused to do so.

Instead, he merely held her gaze and said her name, relishing the opportunity to speak even those two words to her again.

"Miss Hamilton."

"Whoever you are, you must leave. Now. Collier, see this young woman into a cab and back to wherever she came from."

Lady Harriet's harsh tone matched her expression. Will watched her approach Miss Hamilton, as if she meant to push her out the door herself, if necessary.

"I will go, my lady. But first I need Lord Ashdowne to tell me where my sister is."

"Back in Whitechapel, seeking some other protector, I presume." Ashdowne's tone was dismissive, but his gaze continued to rove over every inch of Miss Hamilton's body.

"Freddy, what sordid business have you brought to our door?" Lady Harriet redirected her ire from Miss Hamilton to her brother in the blink of an eye.

"My sister is missing, my lord. She went to visit her friend on Monday evening, but today that young woman told me my sister actually set out on an assignation with you. Here in Mayfair."

Miss Hamilton's accusation was met with silence. Will thought he saw a flash of fear cross Lady Harriet's face and Ashdowne merely continued to stare at Miss Hamilton. When the man finally spoke, his voice dripped with menace.

"Get out. That young woman is a liar. Your sister was a liar. And you have burst into my home uninvited. Take yourself from my doorstep, Miss Hamilton, or I shall have you removed."

Will thought she might protest. Her back was as ramrod straight as the evening before, and her expression held the same look of determination as when she had entered the Ashdowne foyer. But Will noticed that she held her mouth stiffly, and her eyes had grown a fraction rounder. She was scared, and everything in him wanted to protect her.

She took a step back and faltered, tripping over the hem of her own dress. Will approached her more swiftly than he had moved in years and reached out to steady her. His hand clasped her upper arm and she reached up to place her hand over his.

"Let me take you away from here. My carriage is just across the road."

She nodded her head, a small, slight movement, and let him lead her, as if he was a husband escorting his wife, from the Ashdowne's townhouse. As they crossed the threshold the grip of a strong hand encircled Will's arm.

"Selsby, you must stay for supper, old man."

Instinctively Will jabbed his arm back toward Ashdowne, dislodging the man's grasp and nearly knocking him off his feet. He didn't look back to see if Ashdowne fell, but turned instead to Miss Hamilton, pressing her arm gently to guide her as quickly as possible across Grosvenor Square and into his carriage.

CHAPTER 7

ADA WANTED TO SPEAK, TO THANK MR. SELSBY FOR
extracting her from the Ashdowne's townhouse, but she still
felt as wobbly as when she'd stumbled on their marble floor.
She wasn't certain she could speak without her voice shaking
as noticeably as the rest of her body. Was it obvious to Mr.
Selsby within the dark confines of the carriage?

The conveyance was well appointed, but the space inside
was close. Her skirts brushed Mr. Selsby's legs and the heat
of his body warmed her. She could smell the scent of his
soap, hear the steady pulse of his breathing. If only her own
breathing were as steady.

"Your sister—"

"Thank you—"

They spoke over each other, and Ada had a ridiculous
urge to giggle. But nothing about the day had been cause for
giggling. Nancy had known more about her sister's
disappearance than she'd ever admitted. And Ashdowne had
proven less helpful and more odious than she imagined he
might be. The way he had looked at her, the loathing and
hatred she had sensed in his gaze, chilled her to the core.

"Pardon me."

For a man who had come to Whitechapel looking for a woman to satisfy his baser needs, Mr. Selsby was scrupulously polite. Polite and chivalrous. And far too handsome.

"You did not tell me of your sister's plight last evening."

His voice was warm and quiet. They sat so close there was no reason to speak loudly. If she turned her head just so, she could whisper in his ear.

"You didn't know her. I knew you had no idea where she might be."

They were quiet again, and Ada's heartbeat began to steady. The further away they travelled from Lord Ashdowne, the more her fear eased. Something about William Selsby put her at ease too. The man was a conundrum. Her every sense was heightened in his presence and she found it impossible not to catalog each detail about him as she darted furtive glances in his direction—his long, elegant fingers, the scar that marred the skin of his left hand, the fullness of his lower lip, the light golden stubble on his chin and cheeks. She felt safe and secure with him near, as if all would be well, and yet it wasn't true. Nothing would ever be right until she found out what happened to her sister.

His velvety voice interrupted her examination of his profile.

"Is there nothing I can do to help you, Miss Hamilton?"

He turned toward her as he spoke and caught her staring.

It was difficult to be rational when he watched her so intently, let alone speak. "Wh-why do you wish to?"

He looked down at her bare hands gripping the folds of her dress. He moved his own hand a fraction as if he meant to clasp one of hers and then stilled.

She was glad she had not worn gloves and he had not donned his own after leaving the Ashdowne's. She longed to be bold, to move her hands toward his to signal her desire for his touch. As he gazed at her, Ada could not help wanting to know the story behind the sadness she saw in his eyes—the details of every wound, the history of every scar.

"My intentions last evening were far from honorable. I would like to make amends."

"You owe me nothing, Mr. Selsby. And my family, all of us, have worked for as long as I can remember. We do not take charity."

He grinned, a slightly lopsided but utterly charming expression that made Ada long to trace the curve of his mouth.

"I told him you would say that. Ashdowne. I told him you would accept charity from no one."

"He said I would?" The pompous lord seemed to Ada like a man who believed he could buy anyone or anything he wished. Whatever he had given to Beth, whatever she had given to him, Ada knew her sister well enough to believe it had not been about money. Beth had been completely smitten with the man.

"He was wrong." Mr. Selsby's tone was emphatic, as if he believed Lord Ashdowne was wrong about a good many things.

Smitten. Lord Ashdowne had said Mr. Selsby was smitten with her.

"He said you were smitten with me."

It was difficult to meet his gaze as she said the words. She thought she read desire there but feared it was only an imagined reflection of her own feelings. Her heartbeat, which had finally slowed after the debacle at Lord Ashdowne's, kicked up again and she felt her breath coming in quick, tiny puffs.

He lifted his hand and touched her cheek, skimming the backs of his fingers across her skin. His slid his hand lower, to the sensitive flesh of her neck. He stroked her there, his fingers cool against her warm skin, before slipping his hand around the back of her neck and easing her toward him. He looked down at her lips and Ada felt the heat of his gaze as if his mouth was already on hers.

He whispered, "He wasn't wrong about that."

Ada wasn't certain if she leaned forward, he tugged her to him, or he lowered his head. But she knew his lips were warm and soft, easing against hers with a tenderness that melted the worry and fear of the last few days. Ada let her eyes flutter shut and leaned into him, opening to him, savoring the taste and feel of him. He wrapped his arm around her, and she felt protected, surrounded by his heat and scent.

His kiss turned hungry, deeper, and Ada slipped her hands beneath the lapels of his coat, smoothing her fingers against his shirt front, fiddling with a button and the edge of his embroidered waistcoat. She wanted to slip her hands inside his shirt, to feel his flesh against her own.

She pulled away a fraction to catch her breath, and he mistook her meaning and pulled away too. He shifted so that their bodies were not touching, just the brush of her skirt against his trouser legs.

"Forgive me, Miss Hamilton."

"No, I..." But what could she say? That she wanted his kiss? That she had thought of how it would be to kiss William Selsby from the moment she laid eyes on him?

Silence reigned inside the carriage again. Ada longed to speak the truth, but it wasn't proper. The night before she had ascribed her sister's actions to innocence and gullibility. How could she admit to her own desires now?

Ada glanced at Mr. Selsby, his head turned away from her, and noticed through the carriage window that they had entered Whitechapel. She recognized Mr. Mercer's shop front and the familiar windows of Samaritan Hospital as they passed.

Time was short and she had to say something, anything that would make the man look at her again and ease the tension between them.

"Thank you, Mr. Selsby."

She was grateful to him. He'd prevented her from toppling over and making a fool of herself in front of that wretched nobleman and his sister. He had spared her the cost of another hansom cab ride home. And he had given her the first kiss of her life.

Ada felt a tiny burning ache in the center of her chest at the thought she might never see the man again.

Finally he turned to her, but she could not read his expression. He looked grim, yet his eyes seemed as full of fire as the moment before he'd kissed her.

"Miss Hamilton, please call on me if there is anything at all I can do for you or your family. And please take this. I have no use for it."

He lifted a small black box with a green satin ribbon out of his pocket. It looked very much like the box he carried with him the night before.

When she made no move to reach for it, he took her hand, turned it palm up, and stroked it for a delicious moment before placing the box in the cup of her hand.

Moments passed as they watched each other, his hand still touching hers, then the carriage slowed and came to a stop. She heard his coachman call down.

"The Golden Bell, sir."

She knew refusing the gift, whatever was in the small box, was proper, what a lady would do. Considering he had brought it the night before to woo her sister into sin, the object should be odious to her. Yet it was some small part of him she could take away with her—this box and the memory of a kiss she still felt on her lips.

He released her hand and she held very still to stop from reaching for him again.

Mr. Selsby turned as if to exit the carriage, no doubt to help her out, but she unlatched the door on her side, placed her foot on the single step, and hopped down to the cobblestones. It wasn't graceful, but it spared her the embarrassment of allowing him to see how their parting affected her. Her chest burned and tears welled in her eyes. She lifted her chin to prevent them from falling.

"Goodbye, Mr. Selsby."

Ada prayed he did not notice the quaking in her voice. Moving quickly, she crossed toward the Bell and the stairwell leading up to her family's lodgings.

When she closed the door behind her, Ada leaned against it and let her tears fall. Silently so as not to wake the children or her mother, she cried until the weight on her chest lifted. Tears had never been Ada's way—she was the eldest, the one who consoled others when they cried. Now she had shed more tears in past week than in the whole of her life. Her handkerchief was inadequate for the task and she finally slumped into a chair with the sodden scrap of cloth in her hands.

The moment she sat, she felt the sharp edge of the box pressing against her thigh. It had just fit into the pocket of her skirt. She pulled it out and tugged at the green satin ribbon, careful not to let it fall. Vicky would be thrilled to have such a beautiful slip of fabric for her hair.

Ada inched the lid from the box and gasped at the sight of the lovely broach inside. It was a simple design—an oval cabochon surrounded by smaller round cuts—but it was the type of gems that made the piece stunning. Opals, white moon-glow stones, glittered with fire in all the hues of a rainbow. Ada lifted the bauble gently and turned it this way and that, letting it catch the light at various angles so she might enjoy the sparks of green, red, orange, pink, and blue.

"Is it magic?"

Vicky's whispered voice did not startle Ada. If anything she was surprised it had taken the girl so long to come find her after hearing the door open and close. Ever alert, Vicky did not miss much that occurred in their modest, close-quarters lodgings.

"It does seem it. Would you like to see?"

Ada held the gem out and Vicky approached with awe in her honey brown eyes.

She took it and held it reverently in the cup of her hand, stroking the center cabochon with her small finger as if it might grant her a wish.

"It is the prettiest jewel ever." She spoke the words with an innocent sincerity that made Ada smile.

"It just might be."

"He gave it to you, did he not? The man with the pleasant voice?"

"Yes." She told the truth before thinking better of it. Vicky would never meet Mr. Selsby, and Ada was certain she would never see him again.

"Will you marry him then?"

Vicky made it all seem so simple.

"No." Ada tried to keep any tone of sadness from her voice.

"Why ever not? He has given you this precious jewel."

Vicky held the broach up like an offering, and it gleamed in the light of the oil lamp on the corner table. It was a splendid trinket, but Mr. Selsby had not purchased it with her in mind, nor had he given it to her to convey any special sentiment. He had no use for it, he'd said. Perhaps he merely considered it a form of charity she would accept, despite her denial to the contrary.

In truth, Ada did not know if she would ever marry. Once her training was done at the hospital, she hoped to devote her life to nursing, if she proved competent at the work. As the hospital administration did not permit nurses to marry the decision would be out of her hands.

"Ada?"

"Yes, sweet."

Ada stroked the thick, glossy brown waves of Vicky's hair. She took after their mother with her dark tresses and eyes the color of brandy.

"If you will not marry him, should you return his gift?"

She should. She absolutely should. The broach was of fine quality, the kind a man gave to a woman he admired, the kind a woman would cherish forever. It was wrong to keep it. Mr. Selsby should give it to a woman who could cherish it, and him.

But she had no notion of where he lived. She did not want to know. Seeing him again, even to return the jewel, was unthinkable. Ada's behavior had been unladylike, unseemly. Surely he never wished to see her again. Wasn't his offer of the gem a symbol of that? He wanted her out of his carriage, out of his life, and disposing of his ill-intentioned gift put an end to their short, unusual acquaintance.

"I cannot return it, love. I do not know where to find him."

Vicky had replaced the broach in its black box. She fiddled with it, turning and adjusting the jewel until it sat just so on the dark velvet inside. Her nimble fingers snagged on something at the edge of the box and she pulled it out.

"Perhaps this will help." Vicky grinned as she held out her discovery to Ada.

It was a card, much like the one Ada had taken from Mr.

Selsby's hands the night before. This one looked old. The paper was foxed and discolored at the edges. There was no note scrawled in handwriting, only a printed name and address.

Dr. William A. Selsby
42 Moreton Terrace
London

NOW SHE KNEW how to find him. But where would she find the courage to seek him out?

CHAPTER 8

As she stood gazing at the clean white stucco and pillars framing the midnight blue door of number 42 Moreton Terrace, Ada wished she had simply put the box with the broach in the post and been done with the whole business of Mr. Selsby. Done with his dodgy intentions, his soulful grey eyes, and the searing kiss she would never forget. She lifted her hand to her mouth and could instantly recall the press of his mouth on hers, the taste of him.

It was a lovely kiss, and it might be the only one of her life.

She was a pub owner's daughter from Whitechapel, an aspiring nurse who would turn her back on marriage and motherhood for the chance to help those in need. She was a woman with four decent dresses to her name, more than many of her friends possessed, yet women like Lady Harriet Ashdowne would find the notion of so few garments laughable, if not horrifying. Did such a lady ever wear the same gown twice?

Ah, why worry about her betters? She must do the deed

and be done with it. How satisfying it would be to put a close to the whole matter of Mr. Selsby.

And the broach. The prettiest jewel ever, according to Vicky, whose experience of gems was as limited as Ada's. Yet it was lovely. Ada had taken one last peek at it, and it had sparked colorful fire at her, as if enticing her to keep it.

She forced her feet to take the final steps toward Mr. Selsby's door and lifted the polished brass knocker.

Moments later she heard a voice from the other side, though she could not make out what was said. The feminine lilt of the voice was clear. Good God, did Mr. Selsby have a wife? The thought made Ada's heart thrum in her chest and her legs go weak, as if they were made of mince jelly rather than flesh and bone.

The box was heavy in her hand and her instinct was to leave it, to drop it on his doorstep and flee before the woman on the other side could open the door.

But it was too late. The door swung open and a woman, a tentative smile on her pretty oval face, stood looking at her expectantly.

"Beg your pardon, madam, but this belongs to Mr. William Selsby."

Ada thrust the black box toward the woman, praying she would take it swiftly and ask no questions.

Instead, she merely turned her pale eyes toward the box and then gazed back at Ada, seeming to search her face for answers to questions she had yet to ask.

"Won't you come inside, Miss…?"

No, she did not wish to come inside, but it was impolite to do anything else.

"Ada Hamilton."

"Miss Hamilton, please." She gestured for Ada to enter and took two steps aside so that she might do so.

Lifting her skirt a fraction, Ada stepped over the

threshold, holding her breath, fearing she might see Mr. Selsby around the next corner ensconced with a passel of children.

"I am Mrs. Guthrie. Mr. Selsby is my brother. I was just about to take some tea. Won't you stop and join me?"

She was scrupulously polite, just like her brother. And now that Ada took a moment to truly look at the woman, the resemblance was clear in her high cheekbones, pale eyes—though hers were more blue than grey—and the gold-tipped honey brown of her hair.

There was just a moment of hesitation before Ada capitulated. Resisting Mrs. Guthrie's kind eyes and gentle smile proved impossible.

"I would like that, Mrs. Guthrie. Thank you."

Ada was led to a charming drawing room filled with furniture that appeared more comfortable than stylish, vibrant art in gilded frames, and potted plants adding a touch of green to a table here and a corner there.

"Let me just check on the tea. I won't be a moment."

Left alone, Ada seized the opportunity to study the room more closely. With tall bookcases lining the walls on either side of a marble-fronted fireplace, the room seemed as much study as drawing room. She browsed the titles on the spines and was shocked to find dozens of books on medical topics. One title, *Medicine and the Human Mind*, intrigued her and she had just slipped it from its place on the shelf when the drawing room door whooshed open.

"Am I too late for tea?"

Ada did not turn at first. No need, really. That smooth, steady voice was as familiar to her now as if she had known the man for years.

"Miss Hamilton."

She felt a fool standing with her back to him, but the

desire to see his face again was as powerful as the fear. If she saw him again, could she accept that it was for the last time?

Finally, she turned and they locked gazes.

"Mr. Selsby."

Time passed while they scrutinized each other. Ada had no notion how long. The sun seemed to rise higher in the morning sky, for a shaft of gilding light filled the room, illuminating dust motes and lightening the grey of his eyes.

Then Mrs. Guthrie broke the spell, entering the drawing room door followed by a tall, buxom woman bearing a tea tray so wide her arms nearly stretched the width of the doorframe to hold it.

"Just there, Sally. Thank you." Mrs. Guthrie indicated a low table covered with an embroidered cloth. "Good of you to join us, Will. Miss Hamilton and I were just about to take tea."

Ada could not divine the look that passed between brother and sister, but Mrs. Guthrie seemed to be searching his face as intently as she had examined Ada's moments before.

When they were all seated around the table, Mrs. Guthrie performed the ritual of pouring tea—milk for her, milk and sugar for him, plain for Ada—and they all sat in awkward silence, taking the first tentative sips of the deliciously hot brew.

"I see you have found one of Will's medical texts."

The book she had removed from the shelf lay in her lap, though Ada was so startled by Mr. Selsby's appearance at the door she hardly remembered taking it from the bookcase.

It was Mr. Selsby's? There was only one reason a man would require so many books on medicine.

"Are you a doctor, Mr. Selsby?"

"He was going to be. Still could be if he put his mind and

energies to it. Papa was a doctor, you see, and his dearest wish was for Will to follow in his footsteps."

"That was always my intention. But—"

"But when he entered the army, he did not go as a doctor. He wanted to fight, you see. He wanted to be a soldier."

"I was not yet a doctor when I entered the army. I was…"

"A young fool?"

"Quite."

There was no enmity between the two, just a good-natured kind of jesting. They grinned at each other over their teacups, but Ada sensed the moment Will turned his gaze back on her.

"You are interested in medicine yourself, Miss Hamilton?" Mrs. Guthrie's drew Ada's attention away from Mr. Selsby, whose nearness was beginning to turn her thoughts to mush.

"I am a probationary nurse at the Samaritan."

"Well done, Miss Hamilton. A nurse. I am not sure I have the constitution for such a vocation, but I do volunteer at the Bethlem Orphanage. Truth be told, I have long wished to volunteer at the Samaritan, but my brother fears me venturing into the East End on my own. And now Whitechapel is plagued with those unspeakable crimes. So much misery there."

Ada could not help but look directly at Mr. Selsby upon that pronouncement. Whitechapel was too dangerous for his sister, it seemed, but not for the women whose company he wished to procure with flowers and baubles. For a woman he kissed in his carriage.

She held his gaze a moment as she spoke before turning her attention to his sister. "I live in Whitechapel, Mrs. Guthrie. I am afraid some of us cannot avoid the misery, though I am glad to see a bit of it alleviated at the hospital."

"Of course you are. What good work you must do, and where it is most needed. My mother served as a kind of nurse in my father's practice, and I have long thought Will would need such assistance when he finally starts his own practice. Would you ever consider such a post, Miss Hamilton?"

"Kate." Will's tone was chastising, but Mrs. Guthrie's expression was seemingly guileless.

Ada's cheeks began to warm and she feared they'd gone as red as her hair. Mrs. Guthrie was matchmaking, and neither she nor Mr. Selsby could mistake her intent. But why ever would the woman wish to match her brother with a nurse in training from Whitechapel? Their home, their clothes, Mr. Selsby's profession—everything about them indicated both could do much better in marriage than to consider anyone from the miserable East End.

"Do we need more biscuits? Let me just go see." Mrs. Guthrie turned an angelic grin on Ada and then her brother in turn before exiting the room.

"I am sorry about my sist—"

"Forgive me for intrud—"

On a short acquaintance, they seemed to have developed a terrible habit of speaking at precisely the same moment.

"We seem to apologize to each other a good deal." It was the baldest truth, but Ada wondered if she was being impolite to speak it.

"Indeed."

"I only came to return your broach."

He sat forward and Ada feared he might touch her. She ached for him to touch her.

"You do not like it."

"It is stunning. Simply the loveliest jewel I have ever seen."

He ducked his head and she could see that he was smiling.

"Then you should most definitely have it." He looked up

at her, his expression serious. "For you are the loveliest woman I have ever seen."

Ada stood. Every impulse urged her to flee. His compliments were too much, the ardent look in his eyes too potent, and her skin turned feverish the closer he drew near.

She walked to the bookshelf and replaced his book where she had found it, letting her finger trail down the embossed lettering on the spine.

"Has there been any word of your sister?"

Her sister. Beth. For the space of half an hour she had not even thought of her. That is what Mr. Selsby and his too-fine world did to her. The comfortable atmosphere of Moreton Terrace made her momentarily forget the grime and poverty, the need and misery of Whitechapel. The pub had provided her family with a decent living, but she knew her neighbors and those who relied on the Samaritan Hospital struggled in ways she could only imagine. And those women who were victims of the Whitechapel madman. The Mr. Selsbys and Mrs. Guthries of the world read about their torment and it would color their view of the East End forever. And she would be painted with the same brush.

"No, nothing, and the matter is none of your concern, Mr. Selsby. Please thank your sister for the tea and hospitality. I must be on my way."

Ada made for the drawing room door, but Will stood quickly, discarding his cane, and reached for her. His hand closed gently yet firmly around her wrist. Sensation surged like an electric current from the spot where he touched her through every inch of her body, searing her, nearly buckling her knees.

"Ada."

It was the first time he had said her name, and he spoke it as a kind of plea.

She closed her eyes and felt him draw near, his legs

pressed against her skirts, his chest brushing her arm, the heat of his breath caressing the skin of her neck.

"You do not know me, Mr. Selsby."

"I sorely wish to, Miss Hamilton."

She turned her head toward him and their lips were just inches apart. Brazen. Oh, how she wanted to be brazen. To kiss him and touch him, and let the pleasure of it push away every proper thought and nagging worry.

But she couldn't forget who she was, who he was. She could not forget that her sister was nowhere to be found.

"You offered to help me."

He glanced at her mouth before answering.

"Anything."

"Would you speak to Lord Ashdowne about my sister? He must know something regarding her whereabouts."

He took a step back, as if the matter of her sister should cool the ardor between them. But Ada's body still thrummed with an ache she feared only he could satisfy. She still wanted to kiss him.

Instead, she bit her bottom lip and reached inside the pocket of her skirt. The box with the broach felt heavier somehow.

"And please take this back. You should give it to a woman who can cherish it. And you."

He did not reach for the box, nor did he touch her again.

But she still had to go. She set the box on the arm of a chair and strode toward the door. Her footsteps sounded so loud in the quiet of the room.

Don't look back. She could not. She did not.

CHAPTER 9

WILL WAS ROOTED TO THE SPOT WHERE SHE LEFT HIM. A twinge of pain in his leg coaxed him to sit down, but he could not move. She had gone and taken the air, the light, all the comfort of the room with her.

There was so much he wished to say to her. Questions to ask. So much to learn about her. A swell of joy had nearly toppled him when he had rushed into the drawing room and found her there perusing his medical books. She looked so splendidly right in his space, in his home.

Kate's voice echoed from the hallway. "Is Miss Hamilton away so soon?"

Will finally moved, glancing back at his sister and the plate of biscuits in her hand.

"Which county did you visit in order to fetch those biscuits? Yorkshire?"

"I wasn't gone so long."

Will watched his sister resume her chair and take a nibble from one of the fresh biscuits. She had been gone just long enough, and he suspected she might have spent part of the time hovering in the hallway hoping to hear what passed between him and Miss Hamilton. Which, unfortunately, was not nearly enough.

He yielded to the nagging pain in his leg and let his body sink into his favorite chair.

"Long enough for me to chase Miss Hamilton away, apparently."

"Indeed. What the devil did you say to her?"

"Not as much as I wish to."

Kate choked on the biscuit in her mouth and reached for her teacup. After a rather unladylike swig, she shot him her fiercest glare.

"Have you..." She edged forward on her chair, leaned toward him, and lowered her voice to whisper. "Have you done something unseemly to that woman?"

Not as much as I wish to. He couldn't repeat the words to his sister, but his body, still aching from the effect of Miss Hamilton's presence, was a testament to the truth of it.

"I kissed her." Will had never lied to his sister. It was a principle they had agreed upon as children. And it was less about deception than about being wholly plain-speaking with one another. No matter how shocking.

Kate looked indignant. "Here? Just now? You kissed her right here in the drawing room?"

"No, before. In the carriage." Just mentioning the moment brought it vividly to life in his mind. His mouth, his whole body, throbbed with a kind of burning ache at the memory of their kiss. He shifted in his chair and hoped his sister would think it due to his tormenting leg.

Kate slumped back in her own chair and put a hand to her chest as if she was having an attack of the vapors, but his sister was not a woman for feminine theatrics.

He had a moment of real concern before she sat up straight and gazed at him with a conspiratorial grin cresting her face.

"I had almost given up hope the day would come."

What day she referred to escaped him, but he could see she was bursting to say more.

"William Andrew Selsby, you have not spared a glance for a woman for seven years. I thought poor Nerissa Thrumble was going to launch herself into the Thames after all her failed attempts to capture your attention."

"Who is Nerissa Thrumble?"

"You see. Exactly."

Will searched his mind for anyone, any woman, who had made the slightest effort to— Ah, yes, the lady's society friend of Kate's. She had watched him so closely it made him shiver. He felt he was back under his mother's all-seeing gaze.

"Please give my apologies to Miss Thrumble."

"She is happily married to some railroad baron. I'm sure she never spares a thought for you these days."

"What a relief."

"Don't be churlish. When did you become acquainted with Miss Hamilton? And how? It is difficult to imagine you venturing into Whitechapel without a good reason."

It had not been a good reason. It had been desperation. Shame was the only emotion he could identify now, but when he had accepted Ashdowne's wager, it had been born of a kind of fierce need, long denied and more potent due to neglect. He had lived without passion, without gratifying his carnal desires for years, but the prospect of a woman in need of protecting had stoked something primal in him.

Now the tragic truth was the protection Beth Hamilton needed had been too long in coming, and her sister wanted nothing from him. Not protection. Not affection. Not even a broach he had purchased years ago and never given to the woman he hoped to make his wife.

In truth the jewel would have never suited Emilia. Her

preference would have been for rubies or diamonds. The opals required a discerning eye. Modest gems at first glance, they only glittered with kaleidoscopic fire on closer inspection. While Miss Ada Hamilton was a striking beauty at every glance and would have looked delicious dripping in diamonds and rubies, something about the opals suited her. The variegated colors of the gem reminded him of her eyes, which seemed green one moment, blue the next.

"Will? Now who's gone off to some other county?"

"I met her two days ago. In Whitechapel. The rest isn't worth telling."

Kate opened her mouth as if to speak and then closed it again, but she watched him, squinting her eyes a bit as if trying to see more. She opened her mouth again. And closed it.

"What? Say what you wish to say. We have never been coy with one other."

"You looked so pleased to find her here."

Will could not deny that. "Yes."

"If your intentions are honorable toward her—"

"Kate." Will lifted his hand, as if the simple gesture could prevent her from meddling.

"I was only going to suggest that you call on her again. Or invite her to call here for tea. I barely had a moment to speak to her, after all."

Miss Hamilton did not wish to see him again. The finality of their parting was clear. She had returned the broach. She had not looked back.

"She does not wish to further our acquaintance."

He should explain to Kate about Ada's sister, about the whole sordid business with Ashdowne. But he could not find the words. And he feared telling her would mean she might never let the matter rest.

"More's the pity."

It was a pity, though the word seemed inadequate to match the stitch of pain in his chest at the thought he would never see Ada again, never touch her, never know her as he wished to. To cherish her. That was what she had said he should do—find someone to cherish him. Yet she was the one who deserved to be cherished, and he wanted to be the man to do it.

* * *

"GOOD GOD, Selsby, you just can't keep away. Must be my excellent brandy. Shall I pour you a splash?"

Will did not wish to drink, and that was a new impulse. He considered whether drink might loosen Ashdowne's tongue, but decided clouding his own reason was not worth whatever could be gained by partaking with the man.

"No, thank you, Ashdowne. I do not wish to take up too much of your time."

He did not wish to spend one more moment with the man than was necessary.

"I still cannot locate the woman we wagered for." Just speaking the words left a sour taste in Will's mouth. "No one has seen her since Monday last."

"Has she still not turned up? Her new benefactor must be keeping her under lock and key."

Ashdowne's smile was grotesque, more like a viper baring its fangs than a man expressing mirth.

"Did you have plans to meet her last Monday?"

"I did not. She threatened to come here, to Ashdowne House, but I put her off. Told her we were closing up house and heading back to Wythorpe. The season's over. Truth is we should have gone back months ago."

Will recognized the name Wythorpe as the Ashdowne's country estate in Derbyshire.

"Do you think she would try to make her way there? To find you?"

"To Wythorpe?" The notion seemed impossible for Ashdowne to even contemplate. "How the devil would she get there, Selsby? She doesn't have a farthing to her name. And it is a bit too far to walk."

"I thought you gave her money."

"I gave her gifts! And my time. I gave her plenty."

Will stood abruptly, ignoring the twinge in his leg. He did not wish to waste another word on Ashdowne. But it seemed the man wasn't done with him.

"There are plenty of whores in Whitechapel. Even after that madman is done culling a few, there will be plenty more."

It was clear women meant nothing to Ashdowne, their lives even less precious than his collection of stuffed beasts. Will glanced around Ashdowne's study, taking in the array of dead animals adorning every wall. In that moment, he determined it would be the last time he ever saw the man or his morbid collection.

As he took one last look at Ashdowne's lupine smile, a horrific thought struck Will. Did he stand across from a man capable of the kind of horrors being perpetrated in Whitechapel?

CHAPTER 10

THE HECTIC BUSTLE OF SAMARITAN HOSPITAL'S ADMITTING room overwhelmed Will from the moment he crossed the threshold. The sound of so many people—some crying, others moaning in pain—reminded him of the field hospital he had been taken to after his injury at Kandahar.

The smell of carbolic was different though. While they had striven for cleanliness in the field, a makeshift army tent hospital was simply not as well equipped as the efficient machine Will observed before him. Chaos reigned momentarily when a large group of injured men rushed in after an omnibus accident, but Will noted how each man was quickly assessed and sent off to the appropriate ward. Within moments the nurses had reasserted order to the admittance process.

An intense, dark-eyed woman in a starched white nursing costume approached him and asked about his complaint, all the while scanning him from head to toe, as if seeking his injury. He saw her eyes snag on his cane and then catalog the scar on his hand before she met his eyes again.

"Afghanistan or Africa?"

The diminutive woman had the deductive abilities of Sherlock Holmes, it seemed.

"Afghanistan, but it is no physical complaint that brings me to the Samaritan."

This seemed to frustrate her, and she tipped back on her heels and looked up at him with far less interest than the moment before.

"The administrative offices have a separate entrance around the corner, sir. We are here to serve the sick and wounded."

"And you clearly do it admirably."

This seemed to mollify her somewhat and she let loose the minutest grin of appreciation.

"I am here to speak to one of your probationary nurses. Miss Ada Hamilton."

Fear, unmistakable and raw, shadowed her eyes.

"Nurses may not have gentlemen callers of any kind, sir."

"It is regarding her sister, and I thought she might wish to know immediately."

The woman chewed on her lip and then looked back at the line of patients behind him, clearly torn between propriety and her eagerness to rid herself of him and get on to the people who truly needed her help.

"Sit yourself there, and I will fetch the matron to speak with you."

Will glanced at his pocket watch some time later and was surprised to see that nearly one half of an hour had passed before a stern-faced woman dressed in black from head to toe marched toward him from a hallway off the admitting room.

"I am Matron Marley. I understand you wish to speak with me, sir."

Will rose as gracefully as his stiff muscles allowed. The

woman was so tall their eyes were on a level when he stretched to his full height of just over six feet.

"Thank you for your time, Matron. Truth be told, I came to speak with Miss Ada Hamilton. I understand she is a probationary nurse at the hospital and works here during the week."

"Follow me, please."

Will watched the woman stalk away as if the question of him following her was a forgone conclusion. He did not wish to follow her. He only wished to see Ada and tell her his suspicions about Beth after his meeting with Ashdowne.

Matron Marley waited for him inside a surprisingly sumptuous and neat-as-a-pin office outfitted with a massive cherry wood desk and bookshelves stacked with medical journals and ledgers. An impressive painting of the Samaritan Hospital, completed when it was recently constructed and still pristine, dominated the wall behind her desk.

"My I ask your name and interest in Miss Hamilton, sir?"

"Yes, of course. My name is Selsby, and I believe I may have some useful information pertaining to Miss Hamilton's sister."

"The girl who's gone missing?"

He nodded and an expression of real distress passed over the woman's face before her expression returned to the same grim set of mouth and eyes.

"That is tragic. I do hope they find her safe and sound. But I must inform you that Miss Adaline Hamilton is no longer in the hospital's employ. She was dismissed just this morning. And I must say the incidence of a gentleman calling upon her this afternoon…" She indicated Will with the tilt of her head. "Well, it makes me even more certain about my decision."

"I do not have a long acquaintance with Miss Hamilton,

but I suspect you have lost a fine nurse. Why was she dismissed?"

"That is not a matter I am at liberty to divulge. Perhaps Miss Hamilton would care to enlighten you."

* * *

WILL WASN'T LOOKING FORWARD to his next encounter with The Golden Bell's less than friendly giant of a barkeep. The man had begrudgingly served him a drink after his first meeting with Miss Hamilton, but Will suspected it was just because the barman realized Will would soon be out the door.

The pub was crowded for a Monday afternoon, but the burly man seemed to notice Will the moment he crossed the threshold. The man's look was no more welcoming, and this time the giant left his post behind the bar and approached Will.

"You 'ave no business 'ere, my *lord*." The man spoke the word *lord* as if it was the most offensive of curses, as if he was calling Will the Whitechapel murderer and every other kind of monster.

"I am no lord. And my business here is with Miss Ada Hamilton."

Will took a step forward and sidestepped the man, hoping to bypass him completely. But a heavy arm, as thick as the trunk of healthy tree, shot out, not touching him but preventing him from passing.

"That lady is already crying 'er eyes out over yer meddling and lies."

Will remembered how Ada had cried over her sister the first night he'd met her. He suspected she had shed many tears in the last week, and he was determined to alleviate her misery in the only way he could. She may not wish to know him as he wished to know her, but he would help her find her sister.

"I must speak with her. About her sister."

At those words, the man lowered his arm, though he continued to glare at Will as he made his way past him. Will suspected the man watched him all the way up the stairs to the Hamilton family's lodgings.

He rapped on the door only once before it creaked open and a child, eyes red rimmed and sad, opened the door to him.

"Hello. Might I speak with Miss Ada Hamilton?"

Will was shocked when the child smiled at him, a wide, genuine expression that lit up her small face.

"You're the man with the pleasant voice."

"Vicky, come away from the door, dear."

Ada did not look as though she had been crying. She looked lovely, and the gaze she directed at Will set his body alight—the same sizzle of heat he always felt when she was near.

"Please come in, Mr. Selsby."

Will was surprised at the ease with which she invited him into her home. He had feared she might turn him away.

He entered the same family living area where he had first met Ada. She shooed her sister off into another room and offered him tea before they seated themselves at a table in the corner. A delicately woven white doily covered the table and a small vase of wildflowers, blue cornflowers, added a homey touch to the space.

She looked at him expectantly with eyes as vibrantly blue as the flowers and Will began.

"I spoke with Lord Ashdowne. If your sister was determined to find him, it seems she may have gone to—"

"Derbyshire."

"You already knew."

She grinned but he saw no amusement in her now greener than blue eyes.

"My mother told me today that Beth confided in her regarding her relationship with Lord Ashdowne."

She paused and Will could sense her weighing how much to say to him and how much she should shelter her sister.

"Beth told my mother that she was with child." She looked down as she said the words, as if shame for her family prevented her from meeting his gaze.

Will longed to reach for her, to reassure her, but he knew propriety demanded he keep his urges to himself.

"Mother says Beth intended to seek out Lord Ashdowne in Derbyshire, at his family's estate. She cannot recall the name of it."

"Wythorpe."

"I must go there. I must find out what's happened to her."

"Then let me accompany you." The words were out of his mouth before any thoughts of propriety or decorum could restrain them. His desire to be near her, to help her, overrode every other impulse.

She had been sitting beside him, leaning toward him, but upon hearing his offer she stood and began pacing the length of the narrow room.

A gentleman would apologize. But propriety be damned.

"The Samaritan Hospital has dismissed me." She stopped pacing to gaze at him, as if waiting for his reaction.

"I called there. I spoke to Ashdowne and wanted to share my suspicions with you immediately. Matron Marley informed me of your dismissal. I fear I might have made the whole matter worse by calling on you."

She sighed, concern creasing her brow.

"Did she tell you why?"

"She would not."

He could not imagine what she might have done to merit such treatment.

"Lady Harriet is a patron of the hospital, it seems. She sent a letter to the administration requesting my removal from the nursing staff." Ada pulled a folded piece of paper from her skirt, unfolded it, and held it out to him.

Will reached for the paper, expecting to read Lady Harriet's letter, to learn what the woman might have written to lose Ada her position at the hospital. Instead he read a letter addressed to Ada informing her that she had passed her examinations.

He looked up to find her watching him intently.

"The letter arrived in the post today."

"Well done, Miss Hamilton."

She smiled and the beauty of it lit up the room. At least for a moment, the pleasure she felt at her accomplishment outweighed any disappointment over the loss of her position at the Samaritan.

But curiosity nagged at him.

"Lady Harriet. What could she have said?"

Will was sorry to have spoken the words, for Ada's smile faltered, and she shied again, unable to meet his eye.

He approached her, and she finally tilted her head up to look at him. His breath came faster and his heartbeat hitched, sounding the tattoo of a drumbeat in his ears. She affected him like no other woman he had ever met.

Her voice was quiet, almost as if she didn't wish him to hear the words she spoke.

"She informed the administration that I am Lord Ashdowne's doxy."

Her gaze did not waiver from his as she said the word, and she tilted her chin a fraction, as if daring him to look away, as if he might believe Lady Harriet's claim.

But it was nonsense. The Ashdowne siblings seemed

determined to bring misery to the Hamiltons, and it enraged him.

Will moved to retrieve his hat. Surely there was something he could say to Matron Marley to convince her to reinstate Ada. He would deal with Lady Harriet Ashdowne later.

As he turned, he felt Ada's hand on him, small but firm against his coat sleeve.

"Where are you going?"

"To speak to Matron Marley."

"No. It's for the best. You needn't speak to Matron Marley."

The shock of her touch nearly equaled his surprise at her calm regarding the situation.

"You no longer wish to be a nurse?"

Her answer was instant and emphatic. "Yes, very much, but most of all I wish to find my sister. My worry for her consumes me. I am little use as a nurse or anything else until I find her."

Ada smiled at him then—a tender, affectionate expression that stole his breath. "But thank you."

Beyond her beauty and strength, Will glimpsed a woman who looked at him and saw more—more than a wounded man, more than a wretch who had come to Whitechapel for dishonorable reasons. Her gaze searched him, sifted his very soul, and seemed to find something there worth cherishing.

CHAPTER 11

"IS HE A LORD AS WELL THEN?"

Her mother's words echoed in Ada's mind as she settled into the plush first class train carriage and knew the first moments of contentment she'd felt in days. Taking action, going to look for Beth, felt right. And she was not alone. Whatever his reasons, however long he would abide with her, Mr. Selsby was her ally, and one she sorely needed.

Looking around at the details of finely-stitched upholstery, polished wood and brass, and the pretty little blanket that had been provided to warm her, she felt a bit like a grand lady. And it was easy to imagine Mr. Selsby as a lord. It wasn't just to do with his fine clothing and proper manners. Despite whatever injury caused him to rely on his cane and stiffen in pain when he thought no one was looking, he carried himself with an air of confidence and authority that, Ada noticed, made other men make way for him. He and his sister had mentioned his time in the army, and Ada thought he must have commanded men.

He certainly commanded her attention. Though they had the carriage to themselves at the moment, Mr. Selsby had very properly chosen to sit across from Ada rather than by her side. Her disappointment at not having him near was only alleviated by the prospect of studying him as he read *The Illustrated London News.*

She'd noticed his hands the first night she met him, and not just because of the scars. His fingers were long and elegant, and she imagined they would have served him well as a surgeon, if that was what he'd hoped to be. She could easily imagine him as a doctor. Beyond the pain she saw in his eyes, there was kindness. And as Vicky constantly reminded, he had a very pleasant voice, just the kind to put a wary patient at ease.

Though he sat up, back straight, his long legs encroached across the space between them, and Ada relished the feel of them pressing against her skirt. She inched her boots out toward him, her feet on either side of his. The desire to touch him, to draw closer to him, was overwhelming.

He moved the newspaper in his hands and she could finally glimpse his eyes over the edge. Gaze moving over the lines of type, he did not seem nearly as distracted by her presence as she was by his. If only he would lower the newspaper a bit more, she could study his lips. Though they would prove the most distracting of all. She knew what his lips could do.

"My sister sometimes studies me as fixedly." He lowered his newspaper and folded it neatly before setting it aside. "Usually when she thinks I've been up to something dastardly and is determined to suss it out."

"Are you often up to something dastardly?"

He grinned, the movement revealing charming dimples on each side of his face. Ada had studied the anatomy of the human body enough to know it was impossible, but she was certain her heart flip flopped in her chest.

"Not as often as she thinks I am. Not as often I used to be."

It was hard to believe a man with such beautiful eyes could ever be dastardly. Despicable acts were best left to men like Ashdowne and the monster they called the Whitechapel Ripper.

"You're reformed then."

Ada meant her words to be taken lightly, but Will turned his head toward the train car window and looked out onto the rain-soaked landscape beyond. A ghost of a grin still curved his mouth, but his eyes were contemplative.

"Let's just say I have learned my lesson."

He turned his gaze back to her, and Ada felt the same enveloping heat he had stoked the first night she met him. He looked into her eyes, but she felt him deeper, as if he could reach inside and explore all the thoughts and feelings she kept hidden.

"I don't think you have."

This provoked a stunning smile. It made him look rakish, as if naughty deeds were not foreign to him at all.

"No? What makes you say so, Miss Hamilton?"

"Ada." It was so forward, too much familiarity for a man she had only known for a handful of days, but she wanted that intimacy with him. She wanted to hear him say her name. "Please call me Ada, Mr. Selsby."

"Ada." Though her name consisted of two short syllables, he made it sound effusive, a lavish confection he planned to savor. He leaned in, repeated her name huskily, more quietly than any word he had said to her so far. "Ada, you must call me Will. And you must tell me why you think I have not learned my lesson."

Her clothes had fit perfectly a moment before, but now they made her body itch. The heat in her limbs, the sense of melting, fired her cheeks. Ada clutched her dress with both hands, needing to keep them busy so that she did not reach for him. She wanted to provoke him, wanted him closer.

"Because you are taking a train journey with an unmarried woman. Alone."

He looked down, seeming to study the folds of her dress, noticing her hands clutching the fabric.

"I am better behaved than you know, Ada." He looked up slowly as he spoke, letting his gaze trail over her lap and up the row of buttons on the front of her blouse, hesitating at her mouth, and finally meeting her gaze. "There is so much more I would like to do with you."

She had done it now. Whatever threshold of propriety separated them, kept them from touching each other, tasting each other, stripping away clothing and artifice and manners and seeking the pleasure they would surely find together—that threshold was crossed. And she didn't want to go back.

Ada reached for him, aching to kiss him. She touched the firm line of his jaw, traced the light stubble with her fingers. But he didn't kiss her mouth, merely turned his head to lay a kiss against her palm.

His hands were busy elsewhere, reaching down, gathering the edge of her skirt and petticoat, lifting them slowly, skimming his fingers along her legs. His hands moved higher, higher—she ached for him to reach the top of her cotton stockings, to feel his fingers against her bare flesh.

"These skirts have been tormenting me all day." He shook his head. "No, not your skirts." Her skirts were bunched around his arms, and he reached under one of Ada's legs, lifting it so that her boot heel rested on the edge of his bench seat. "The thought of these legs, this soft skin. That's what drives me mad."

His left hand closed around her thigh, and she felt his fingertips against her bare skin. He reached higher still, slipping his fingers inside her drawers.

Ada hissed and nearly let out a cry of frustration when Will stopped, as if he meant to release her, as if he feared he had crossed the line.

"Please." She meant to ask him to touch her, to love her and not to stop, but she could only manage the single word.

He kissed her then, his mouth touching hers tenderly at first before he sought more—tasting her, teaching her. Their lips met again and again, drawing more from other every time they touched.

Ada felt his fingers slide further, deeper inside her draws, until they touched the curls at the apex of her thighs.

After another kiss—as deep as she wished his fingers to be, as wet as the moistness between her legs—he pulled back to watch her. Ada bit her bottom lip to hold back the cry she longed to release, and she held still, though she wanted to move. She wanted to push against his finger, feel more, stoke the pressure building inside her body.

"Should I stop, Ada? We are treading close to the edge."

She moved then, to show him, to tell him with her body that she wanted him, wanted all of him. "Don't you dare stop."

He moved and the pleasure-pain of his finger breached her core, claiming her as no man ever had. He kissed her as he drew closer, leaning into her, his finger sliding inside her slick heat.

Ada relished the press of his body over her, the slip of his finger inside her, and she wanted more. With one hand she reached for his lapel, tugging at it, needing him as close as she could have him, and she moved her other hand around his neck, raking her fingers through the hair at his nape.

A shudder began to rock her. She felt it building, igniting at every point their bodies met, and swelling out, down her legs, her arms, tickling up her spine, until she trembled in his embrace. Waiting. Just on the precipice.

He touched her deftly, each movement more delicious, pushing her further. He released her mouth and moved his lips across her cheek, up near the shell of her ear.

"Let go, love. I'll be here to catch you."

When his teeth grazed the tender skin of her earlobe, Ada let go—falling, soaring, trembling and crying out, caring nothing for who might hear her.

And when she could breathe again, could think again, he was there, just as he promised. He'd given up any pretense of propriety and sat beside her, holding her, his lips pressed to her temple.

Ada turned so that she might fit more snuggly against him and realized he was trembling, just as she had been moments before.

Pulling back, she gazed up at him and he grinned down at her, and not just with his mouth but with his eyes. It was the first time she looked at Will and did not discern sadness in his gaze.

The words on the tip of her tongue were straight from her heart but Ada feared letting them out. Only days before she would have considered a man such as William Selsby far above her station, but now she was closer to him—more intimate with him—than she had ever been with anyone in her life.

"That was—"

"You look—"

Ada smiled and Will shook his head. They must learn to take turns speaking, it seemed.

The thought made Ada consider the future and a wave of anxiety crashed in, washing away the moment of ease and contentment. Would there be a future with Will? It was difficult to consider any future at all. In her mind's eye, all she saw was Beth's face. How could she plan her own future when she did not know her sister's fate?

CHAPTER 12

W<small>YTHORPE WAS EVEN GRANDER THAN</small> A<small>DA PREDICTED, AND IT</small> was bewitching to the eye with its many windows lit from within. The November night was cold and she could see a massive fireplace blazing through a immense window to the left of the front doors. It made the too large country house seem inviting, though she knew the Ashdownes would never offer her anything like hospitality.

Will led her to stand on the doorstep beside him, but she hung back, out of sight behind his tall frame, fearing her presence would get them turned away altogether.

After a brief wait, a gentleman dressed in the fine kit of a rich man's servant opened the door.

"Good evening, my name is William Selsby. I realize the Ashdownes are not at home, but I wonder if I might speak with the butler or housekeeper here at Wythorpe."

Ada peeked around Will's arm to see the young man at the door raise his eyebrows and shoot Will an assessing gaze before replying.

"Lord Frederick Ashdowne and Lady Harriet Ashdowne are at home, sir. Shall I inform them you have come...to call?" The young man looked up at the night sky, as if to imply calling at such a late hour was akin to heresy.

Will glanced back at Ada with a questioning expression. Neither of them had expected the Ashdownes to be at home. Only days before Ada had confronted the siblings in their London townhouse. The brother and sister must have decamped shortly afterwards.

Ada shrugged, less helpful, perhaps, than Will wished her to be.

"Yes, if you would be so good. Thank you."

Will pointed his cane ahead of him to indicate Ada should precede him into Wythrope's massive entry hall, and both of them followed the young man into a drawing room to the right of a grand double staircase.

When the young man left them alone in the room, Will reached his hand out to Ada and she grasped it quickly, grateful for his strong, steady presence. If he was concerned about another confrontation with Ashdowne, it did not show on his face or in his gaze. Yet he seemed to sense the fear that made it difficult for her to stop shivering.

"You have nothing to fear from Ashdowne. We shall face him together."

Ada drew closer to Will. After what they had shared on the train, she was finding it difficult to stay her hands from touching him at every opportunity. She turned her gaze up to his face and focused on his cool grey eyes. The emotion she saw there both ignited and soothed her.

He bent his head down and her mouth tingled, anticipating his kiss, but movement and sound beyond the drawing room door made them pause.

Ada heard women's voices and laughter, their giggles high-pitched and harsh to her ears. One woman's voice was louder, her words clear.

"No, this one's the sitting room, I am certain. Is it not far too easy to get turned around with so many rooms?"

When the doorknob began to turn Ada pulled away from Will. Propriety dictated she had no right to touch him, no matter how she wished to. But he held her fast, allowing her to step away but not releasing her hand. His gaze never wavered from her face, even when the woman who stepped across the drawing room threshold cried out his name.

"William!"

Ada thought the woman's laughter was shrill, but it was nothing to the sound of her scream. And she did truly scream Will's name.

When both she and Will turned their heads toward the sound, Ada sensed Will's shudder before he released her hand. His eyes had gone wide, as wide as eyes of the woman who stared at him from the doorway. She was a striking figure, tall and willowy, with auburn ringlets framing her face and cascading down around her shoulders.

"Is it truly you? I cannot believe it. They told me you would lose your leg. And your arm. They told me you might never walk again. Never be whole again."

The woman rambled on as she approached them, her elegant gown fluttering around her. She walked right up to Will, as close as Ada stood to him, then closer, and reached her hand up toward his cheek. She paused just before touching him, as if she feared he was a phantasm.

"But you are whole. Whole and well and as impressive as ever." She touched him then, her fingertips grazing his cheek and tracing a line toward his temple, and Ada saw him flinch. "You always did have the most beautiful eyes."

The woman did not seem to notice Ada's presence at all. Her whole focus was on Will's face, but when she stepped one pace forward, as if she meant to do more—kiss him?—

the woman who had followed her into the drawing room called out.

"Emilia!"

Her companion's tone was harsh, scolding, and seemed to bring Emilia out of a kind of daze.

Watching Will, Ada thought he looked relieved Emilia had stopped touching him, stopped moving toward him. He reached for Ada's hand again and she took his, stroking his skin and feeling the ridge of scars under her fingertips.

Ada whispered to him. "Who is that woman?"

"Come away, dear." The woman who accompanied Emilia was tugging at her arm, trying to extract her from the scene.

But Emilia, now weeping and sniffling, continued to ramble, her words directed at Will.

"I never wished to marry him. Even with all his titles and houses and the castle… I would have married you."

"My goodness, Emilia, I wondered where you had got to."

Ada recognized the imperious tone of Lady Harriet, the woman who had lost her a position at the hospital, an appointment she had worked so hard to earn.

When Lady Harriet saw the assembled group and noted the tears streaming down Emilia's face, she turned pale before directing an angry gaze at Ada and then Will.

"I don't recall extending you an invitation, Captain Selsby. You or your…companion." Lady Harriet turned her attention to the woman called Emilia. "Duchess, come away from all of this."

Ada was stunned to hear that the woman who cried for Will was a duchess, even higher in rank than Lady Harriet, if Ada had her lords and ladies and titles right.

Will had not spoken to Emilia. Ada had barely seen him turn his gaze in the woman's direction, but then he glanced at Emilia once before speaking calmly and quietly to Ada.

"We should depart. There is no help for us here."

Relief swept over Ada. She wanted nothing more than to leave Wythorpe, to turn her back on the Ashdownes and the woman who watched Will with a tearful, longing gaze. She was curious about the woman but knew her questions were better left for another time.

He led her, drawing her along, her hand in his.

Lady Harriet spared them one last disdainful glance and they had almost made it to the threshold when Emilia broke away from the woman who embraced her and launched herself at Will.

He turned his body to shield Ada, and then craned his head back, offering his first words to the woman who was so affected by the sight of him.

"Miss Copley. Emilia. What was between us is in the past. Let us leave it there."

He nodded, a curt gesture of forced politeness to Lady Harriet, and then strode out of the drawing room, across the entry hall, and out the doors of Wythorpe. He seemed to have forgotten that he even carried a cane and walked so quickly that Ada struggled to match his long strides.

He slowed his pace when they began ascending Wythorpe's long drive toward the path that would lead them back to the village. The gentleman who had driven them from the train station to Wythorpe for a shilling was likely snugged up in his home, and Ada could not blame him. It had turned so cold their breaths puffed out in front of them as they walked.

Moonlight illuminated the road and the grim look on Will's face. Ada wished to stop him, ask him about the encounter in the Ashdowne's drawing room, but it was too chilly to stop on the road.

Will must have sensed her examining him, as he turned to her and offered her a grin that belied the sadness in his eyes.

"Are you all right to walk? It is at least a mile yet to the village inn. Here, take my coat." Will started to remove his long woolen coat, but Ada stopped him.

"No, I am well. I quite enjoy walking."

At Ada's words, Will's expression changed. He smiled and it carved dimples in his cheeks, lighting up his face. For a moment it was if the emotional scene at Wythorpe had never happened.

"Do you? In the dark? And the cold?"

His eyes glowed in the moonlight and Ada could not help but speak from her heart. "With you, yes. I suspect I would always enjoy a promenade with you."

It sounded silly, but it seemed to please him. He stopped and lifted his arm, offering to enfold her in his coat. Ada's height allowed her to fit neatly by his side, just under his outstretched arm, and he wrapped his great coat around both of them. They started walking again, awkwardly until they came to match each other's pace, and Ada noticed that he hardly used his cane, barely touching it to the ground with each step.

They didn't speak again until they reached the village tavern. Ada took a seat at a table near the fireplace and Will approached the publican. She heard him inquire about a meal and lodgings for the night.

The man behind the bar had a deep, blustery voice that carried across the confines of the cozy taproom. "Aye, I have a room to suit you and your fine lady there. Seat yourself before the fire and my missus will bring you both a bowl of mutton stew."

Talk of food made Ada's stomach rumble, and the mention of a shared room made other parts of her body tingle. Will could hardly let the innkeeper know they were unmarried without causing a good deal of fuss. Still the notion of spending an evening alone with him made her throat dry.

He approached the table and Ada felt suddenly nervous. She was eager to ask him about the woman at Wythorpe, and she yet she feared the answers. Despite his parting words to the woman, Ada could not help acknowledging there must have been feelings between them. The woman's reaction had been extreme and her emotions seemingly heartfelt. Was Will's heart as affected?

Before she could form a question, the innkeeper's wife approached with a tray and settled two steaming bowls of stew, slices of bread and cheese, and a knob of butter before them. Her husband followed on her heels and placed a pint of ale before Will and a cup of tea in front of Ada.

As they ate Ada found herself wishing for a bit of ale herself, but she didn't want to shock Will anymore than she had with her behavior on the train.

"Would you care for a sip?"

He lifted his pint toward her, apparently reading her mind.

"I have my tea."

"Every time you take a sip of your tea, Miss Hamilton, you stare longingly at my ale."

"Do I, Captain Selsby?" Ada took a sip of tea, keeping her gaze on Will's face, attempting to disprove his claim about her lust for his ale.

He took a generous gulp in response and Ada licked her lips, more affected by the movement of muscles across his throat than by thirst for his drink.

After a few moments of silence, she resolved to ask about the woman, but just as she opened her mouth to speak, Will took a breath as if he meant to express himself too. Ada closed her mouth and waited.

"I'll return to Wythorpe in the morning."

A burning ache started in the center of Ada's chest. If he returned to Wythorpe, would he encounter the woman who preferred him over a duke? She was beautiful and elegant, and possessed wealth and a status so different from Ada's.

"I shall try the servant's entrance this evening. The housekeeper, even the cook, will know if Beth has ever been at Wythorpe."

Of course he would keep his focus on their true purpose for venturing to Derbyshire. Yet after being at Wythorpe, Ada couldn't imagine Beth there. The girl would rarely even visit Ada at the Samaritan Hospital, insisting that the building was too imposing. Even if she had made her way to the Ashdowne's estate, they would have turned her away. Would she have confided in anyone where she might go next?

Beyond the endless worry for her sister, the question of where she had gone, another question nagged at Ada's mind. "What about Emilia?"

For what a seemed an endless pause, Will did not respond. He stared at his mostly uneaten bowl of stew, not meeting Ada's gaze.

"Perhaps we should retire for the evening."

He spoke the words before looking up at Ada. When he did, his gaze was stark, his eyes emotionless and his mouth a harsh line across his face. It was as if another man, one she had not come to know and care for over the previous days, sat staring back at her.

"All right." Ada hadn't meant the two words to come out so quietly, but his change in manner unsettled her.

He stood and started toward the stairs, not looking back to see if she followed. He strode quickly, his boot heels clicking on the pub's weathered floorboards.

As Ada watched him walk away from her, a glint of gold caught her eye. His cane rested against the table. Not only was the new Will grim-faced, he had no discernable limp and apparently required no aid to help him walk.

Ada stood and took a deep breath. Whoever he had become, whatever had caused such a change in his demeanor, tonight she would be sharing lodgings with him.

CHAPTER 13

IF HE HAD NOT HEARD HER FOOTSTEPS ASCENDING THE STAIRS behind him, Will would have turned back. He owed her an apology. He owed her more than that. She was the loveliest, strongest, and most desirable woman he had ever met. And he did desire her, had from the moment he first laid eyes on her. Yet the way he had met her, the circumstances of his visit to Whitechapel, even his loss of control on the train were not honorable. She deserved more—a proper courtship, marriage—and better than a broken man covered in scars.

As he stepped into the inn's snug room, he spied a well-worn chair near the fireplace that would serve as his bed for the night. He approached it but could not sit. Frustration made comfort impossible, and as he heard Ada moving around in the room—laying her cloak aside and filling the wash basin with water—he ached with the desire to touch her, hold her, to offer an explanation for his rudeness in the taproom.

"I'm sorry, Ada."

Speaking to her was difficult, but looking at her proved

even more of a challenge. He feared what he might see in her gaze.

She sat at the foot of the bed, perched there, her back as ramrod straight as the night he had met her. Her eyes glittered like blue flames in the candlelight, and her red hair hung in lustrous waves around her shoulders. Will had never seen such a magnificent sight.

As he watched her, she reached down and brandished his cane.

"You left this downstairs."

His cane was the least of his concerns, an unwelcome reminder of the man he had become.

"Perhaps you do not need it." She cast it back down on the floor with her declaration.

He did not wish to examine how he relied on his cane, but he knew with staggering certainty that Ada Hamilton was what he needed, and his desire for her was like a hunger. The truth of it washed over him, tinged with joy and trepidation in equal measure.

"What I do need is to explain. May I?"

Will indicated the space next to her on the bed and she placed a hand there to indicate her invitation.

When he lowered himself to rest beside her, Will found the warmth and scent of her body a powerful balm. His frustration ebbed, replaced with the urge to confess his feelings, to make Ada Hamilton understand how much he wanted her. But first things first.

"I was betrothed to Emilia Copley, now the Duchess of Marbury, before I left for Afghanistan."

Ada did not move or look at him as he spoke. She had fixed her gaze on the hearth and was so still she might have been holding her breath.

Will yearned to reach for her, but stayed his hand, eager to get his explanation regarding Emilia out so that he might get on to telling Ada of the sentiments weighing on his heart.

"When I returned, nearly eight years ago now, she refused to see me. I wrote to her, called at her family's home, even sent word via a mutual friend. All to no avail. She never informed me she wished to break our engagement, though my intention was to release her from it. In fact, she had married the very same year I returned, just a few months before my arrival in London. But it was for the best. I was in no state to marry, and I was not certain I would ever be."

Will grasped his cane and leaned on it gingerly to stand. Talk of the past, of Emilia's rejection, sent a shooting pain down his leg. Standing seemed to ease it, but he missed the warmth of Ada's body next to his.

Two strides brought him to the fireplace where a few logs still flickered, but the heat offered none of the satisfaction the woman behind him could provide with a single touch.

"She seemed quite affected by the sight of you." Ada's spoke quietly, as if the words were difficult to utter.

Emilia's reaction had shocked him. Seeing her taught him how much he had forgotten about her, as if he was gazing on a stranger, not the woman he had known at all. Though graceful and elegant, nothing about her had stirred him, except to inspire a desire to escape. Her touch had repulsed him, and he had wanted nothing more than to push her hand away.

"Were you?"

Will feared he had missed something Ada had said. He turned to look at her, still sitting primly, her hands folded in her lap, on the edge of the bed.

"Was I?"

"Were you affected by seeing Emilia again?"

The sight of her had brought back memories of pain and regret, but nothing of whatever tenderness he had once felt toward her. Now, here with Ada, he realized he had never loved Emilia, and despite her emotional display, he suspected she had never loved him either. If she had, her love had been a thin, fragile thing, too delicate for the realities of a man marred by war.

"It roused memories."

Ada seemed deflated by his answer. She tilted her head down a fraction, abandoning her stiff posture.

Will approached and resumed his place beside her. He could not resist anymore. He reached for her, grateful she did not pull away.

"Unpleasant memories, Ada. No finer feelings. Nothing like desire."

He swallowed hard. The time had come to risk again.

"Nothing like what is between us."

The wait between his words and her response seemed to stretch out, giving Will time to sift possibilities.

"What is between us?" Ada spoke the words as a question, and Will had only one answer.

"I love you, Ada. And if you'll have me—"

ADA PRESSED HER lips to Will's, cutting off his proposal. She heard the one word that echoed her own feelings, and her heart and soul reverberated with the sentiment. Love— he loved her and she loved him—and nothing more was needed.

Ada kissed him, offering every bit of her heart, her body, all that she was and hoped to be. No more hesitation. No more concern for decorum and propriety.

She slid her hands inside his jacket, unfastened the buttons of his waistcoat, and pushed the fine fabric aside. When she slipped a button on his shirt and slid her fingers underneath to touch his bare chest, he took a sharp breath and broke their kiss.

Will skimmed his lips over her flushed cheek, slid his mouth toward her ear, and began trailing kisses down her neck. His breath was hot on her skin, though the touch of his mouth on her body made Ada shiver.

When Will began working the buttons of her gown, she sighed in relief. Ada yearned to remove every barrier between them, and her clothing was suddenly a heavy, uncomfortable obstruction.

He peeled back her jacket and moved his hands to the frayed ribbon at the neck of her chemise. Much of her clothing was frayed, serviceable but often mended, and most of it well-worn and less than fashionable.

Ada reached up to halt his progress.

"I'm not a duchess."

She heard him chuckle and saw the flash of his smile.

"For which I am most grateful." He attempted to pull at the ribbon, but Ada held his hands fast.

"You are?"

"Mmm." He pulled back and gazed into her eyes. "You see, I am not a duke, and I wish to marry you. If you were bent on being a duchess, where would that leave us?"

Though his tone was teasing, Ada could not shake her concerns, fears that suddenly diluted the pleasure of his touch.

"Emilia is a duchess and she wishes to—"

Will moved his finger to her mouth and then replaced it with his lips. His kiss was deep, engaging all of her senses, eclipsing everything else. She could hardly recall the words she'd meant to say.

Will drew back a fraction and whispered to her. "She is better off where she is." He kissed Ada again, nipping lightly at her lower lip. "And I am exactly where I wish to be."

He set to work in earnest then, unwrapping her like a gift he'd been given. He momentarily abandoned the ribbon of her chemise to free her from her corset, then unhooked her skirt and slid it down her hips. He kissed her as he worked, alternating slow, languorous attention to her lips with hungry nips at her neck, sometimes lifting his head to trace the shell of her ear with his mouth.

Ada wanted him closer; she pulled and tugged at his clothing less skillfully and with far less patience.

Will seemed to catch her urgency and yanked at her petticoat so fiercely the sound of ripping fabric broke into their symphony of moans and heavy breathing.

He stilled and looked abashed. "Forgive me, love. I'll buy you a dozen petticoats."

The true regret in his eyes made her smile. Her petticoat had seen better days, but she knew she had never met a better man.

"Forget my petticoat and kiss me again."

He did. He kissed her and released her from her petticoat and drawers and finally tackled the knotted ribbon of her chemise before slipping his hand inside and cupping her breast. Ada shuddered at the feel of his bare flesh on hers. He kneaded her body gently before tracing his fingertips in circles over the swell of her bosom, drawing ever smaller rings until he captured her firm peak.

She gasped into his mouth as he kissed her. Pushing back the fabric of his shirt, Ada relished the feel of his skin under her hands, the arch of muscle, the smooth curve of his back, even the ridge of scars on his shoulder and lower on the hard swell of his bicep.

It was his turn to pull back, tucking a finger under her chin and lifting her head so they met eye to eye.

"I recall you're not a duchess, but you should know I am

an imperfect man. The circumstances of our first meeting must have taught you that."

Ada opened her mouth to speak but the look in his eyes, as if he needed this moment to express a painful truth, stilled her tongue.

"I am flawed. Scarred." He indicated the scars on his arm. They surrounded a vicious looking gouge in his flesh, now faded, but still quite visible. "Damaged, I'm afraid. Inside and out."

Ada gazed up at him, praying he could read the love she offered him.

"It is quite lucky for you, then." She traced the pattern of his scars, gently, tenderly, as she spoke.

"Lucky?"

"That I am a nurse and not a duchess."

He stood then, pulling her up against him.

"Lucky, indeed."

She felt the insistent ridge of his manhood pressing against her thigh. Emboldened, she reached down to release the buttons of his trousers. When he'd shed the garment, there was no longer any barrier between them. For a moment, Ada merely reveled the in the feel of his body—hard planes and sharp angles—pressed against her curves.

When he led her to the bed and arched over her, covering the length of her body with his own, Ada could not restrain a purr of satisfaction from bubbling up. He felt so right, and their bodies fit together as if they had been made for this moment of joining.

Will kissed and touched her, his hands roving to stroke and knead her skin, stoking a burning ache inside of her.

She felt the press of him, heat and steel between her legs, and bucked against him, eager to ease the ache between her thighs. He responded, bending his head to capture her lips, his tongue plunging into the wet heat of her mouth, as his body rocked into her soft flesh.

Ada moaned into his mouth, not from pain, but from the extraordinary sense of fullness, wholeness, she felt as Will moved inside her. Close—their bodies were so close she felt his heartbeat against her own chest. He thrust with delicious purpose, slow and languid, as if he was savoring her inch by inch. But her need for him was not gentle. It burned her from the inside, from the point where their bodies joined, and ratcheted hotter with every stroke.

She lifted her leg, hooking it around his waist, and urged him deeper, wanting more of him, all of him.

His breath came in rapid gusts across her face as he plunged into her, watching her, his eyes filled with love and desire and the same hunger that fired every inch of her body. As she met his gaze, the hunger built, driving her toward the edge. She arched her back and a shudder built, melting her, consuming her. She reached out, gripping Will's arm, scraping her fingers across his back, and cried out his name. He was still above her, watching her, moving inside her, seeming to revel in her release. Then he bent his head and captured the tight bud of her nipple in his mouth. Ada bucked again and he drove deep, moaning against her breast, as he shuddered with his own completion.

Will lifted his body off of hers and Ada turned to tuck herself against him. He reached down for the quilt folded near the foot of the bed and pulled it over them. A few embers still flickered in the fireplace, offering little warmth but painting the room in an amber glow. Ada glowed too. She felt warmth unfurling inside her body as her breathing steadied. Will's heartbeat was steadying too. She felt it under the flat of her palm as it rested against his chest.

She tipped her head to kiss him, nuzzling his face, and enjoying the brush of stubble against her skin. Ada could not ever remember feeling such a sense of contentment. She was sated and the drowsiness of sleep made her eyes heavy lidded.

As her eyes began to flutter closed, Will's fingers traced a line across her cheek, up toward her temple. He stroked her hair, combing his fingers through, giving her comfort and pleasure and driving her closer to sleep.

Thoughts of Beth assailed her the moment she closed her eyes. She had been so fixed on her own pleasure she had not spared her sister a thought for hours. Guilt and worry coalesced into questions, questions she had been asking for over a week. Where was she? Was she safe? How would they find her?

CHAPTER 14

WILL WOKE TO AN ACHING PAIN IN HIS ARM. STRANGELY, IT was not his injured arm but his other. And it was tucked neatly under the body of a luscious woman. In the sunlight, he noticed her pale skin was freckled here and there, and her long, thick red hair trailed over her body in cunning ways. A curl curved around her neck, a strand had slipped down to trail over her breast, and a long wave of crimson stretched out over her arm.

He traced several strands with the tips of his fingers but was more interested in the smooth flesh underneath. Her nipple peaked when he stroked the tress near her breast and she turned fully onto her back, stretching with a satisfied little moan like a cat after a long nap.

When she opened her eyes and found him watching her, touching her, she looked momentarily flustered and reached to cover herself with the quilt. But Will would have none of it. He kissed her soundly and smiled against her mouth when he felt Ada slip her hand around his neck and pull him closer.

When he broke their kiss, she gave him a serious look.

"Do you think we've missed the first train back to London?"

He guessed they had, but he was confused by her desire for haste. It seemed prudent to question at least a few of the Ashdowne's head servants before leaving Derbyshire.

"Should we not speak to the housekeeper at Wythorpe?"

At the mention of the Ashdowne's family estate, Ada turned her head away. He could not blame her for wishing to avoid another encounter with the aristocrats, yet they had journeyed far to learn of her sister's whereabouts. As yet they had found nothing.

No, not nothing. He had found everything. Ada turned back to him, her marvelous blue-green eyes glowing in the sunlight, and he wanted her with an acute ache, sharper and more vivid than anything he had ever felt in his life.

"You're right. We should do all we can to find her, even if it means seeing Lord Ashdowne again."

Will kissed the tip of her nose, afraid to kiss her mouth for fear he could not stop there. "If we hurry, we can call before the Ashdownes have even risen from their beds."

* * *

THOUGH THE TAPROOM was much the same as Ada recalled it from the night before, she was different. Despite the purpose of their journey and her lingering worry for Beth, Ada perceived a transformation. The world looked brighter, and in her heart she knew an ease, as sense of repletion so sweet she was tempted to doubt it, question it, even fear it. Instead she settled into it, let it flow and surge until she felt the twitch of a smile on her face for no particular reason at all.

As Will approached from the bar where he had retrieved cups of tea for each of them, a woman's laughter echoed against the walls of the pub, mirroring the lightness in her heart and the elation she was beginning to embrace.

The laughter was hearty and then the woman began to shout, good naturedly but vehemently, and Ada nearly fell off her chair.

She shot up, nearly upsetting her teacup, and glimpsed a look of shock and concern on Will's face before she turned toward the sound of the woman's voice and started shouting herself.

"Beth! Beth!"

A head full of red-orange curls dipped out from a room near the pub's bar. "Ada!"

Ada barreled toward her sister.

Beth reached out to embrace her and they spun for a moment, giggling and crying and repeating each other's names.

Ada pulled back and held Beth at arm's length. "My goodness, you look wonderful." She gazed down at Beth's belly. "Are you...?"

"No."

"But you told Mother—"

"She would never have let me come otherwise."

"Beth." Ada said the word in a scolding tone and instantly regretted it. Two minutes in each other's company and she and her sister had fallen into their roles of elder sister and younger.

"Who's the toff?" Beth tipped her chin in Will's direction and Ada looked back to find him watching them. He arched one tawny eyebrow, as if to inquire whether he was wanted, and Ada instantly nodded.

Ada leaned in to whisper to Beth before he reached them. "I very much hope he will be my husband."

Beth reeled back and grinned. "Heavens, woman. I have only been gone the better part of a week."

"Yes, and we're so pleased to have found you."

At the rich baritone of Will's voice, Beth's eyes went wide. She looked him up and down, taking in his tall frame and elegant clothes and looked repentant. After Ada made introductions, Beth began babbling out the story of her disappearance and how she came to be working at the Eagle and Castle Inn in Derby.

When Frederick Ashdowne had discarded her, despite promises of marriage and assurances she would be his countess one day, Beth had determined to rekindle his interest, no matter the cost. She attempted to speak to him at the Ashdowne's London townhouse and was told the family had departed for their estate in Derbyshire.

After telling their mother of her false pregnancy and promising she could secure a real proposal from Ashdowne if she saw him again, Mother had encouraged the girl, even providing the last bit of funds to purchase a train ticket. Ada could not resist rolling her eyes at hearing the full measure of her mother's involvement in the scheme. How could she have feigned worry and allowed Ada and Vicky to stew over Beth's disappearance?

"But why did you not write? Why did you not come back to Whitechapel?"

Ada interrupted Beth's story with her questions, but she needed answers. Will stood quietly, content to listen rather than interfere between sisters.

"I was ashamed, wasn't I? Freddy was not here in Derbyshire. He lied. He lied and lied, and I believed him." Beth pushed out her lip in a pout and Ada saw tears well in her eyes. "I couldn't bear for Mama to know what a fool I'd been. For you to know."

Ada reached for Beth's hand, realizing how small and fragile it was. She had grown thinner in the past week, though she looked otherwise in good health—her eyes bright and a rosy bloom on her cheeks.

She tempered her tone, speaking softly. "Did you never mean to come home to us? To let us know how you fared?"

At the question, Beth's eyes darted back to the room she'd exited when Ada called her name. Ada followed the direction of her gaze and noticed a young man, tall and lanky, with dark hair and eyes. Had he been watching their entire exchange?

Beth motioned to him with her hand and he stepped forward.

Ada noticed that his hair was a rich chocolate shade and his eyes much the same, though a bit lighter, and busy. He glanced momentarily at Will and Ada, but his gaze immediately returned to Beth. Ada knew that look. The boy loved her. And she had the cheek to comment on Ada's hasty wooing!

"Ada, Mr. Selsby, this is Robert Cornforth."

The young man reached out to shake Will's hand and nodded politely to Ada before drawing closer to Beth.

"He has asked me to marry him and I've accepted."

"Beth, that's very sudden." Will turned a raised-brow gaze on Ada the moment the words were out of her mouth. He of all people knew she had no place to chastise anyone about sudden affection, about the rush of sentiment between two people who had known each other a handful of days.

Breathing deeply, she smiled at Mr. Cornforth and then at the man she loved as fiercely as she had ever cared for anyone. Yes, she understood a love that kindled quickly and flashed into flame.

"I wish you both well. Truly, I do. But Beth, won't you come back to Whitechapel with me to reassure Mother and Vicky you are well?"

Will reached a hand toward Ada and rested it possessively on her arm. She relished the weight and heat of his palm.

"Perhaps Mr. Cornforth would wish to come too?"

Mr. Cornforth looked surprised yet thankful to be included in the conversation.

"Aye, indeed, sir. I would like to accompany Beth anywhere she goes."

The sentiment was spoken so plainly, heartfelt and without a trace of artifice, that Ada found it easy to understand how her sister could have become smitten so quickly. Then again, she'd been smitten with Lord Ashdowne too.

Was love so ephemeral, sparking up one day and then burning out only to kindle again, and quickly?

What she knew of Will she could scribble on a single scrap of paper—the facts she had learned about his family, his history, details about his life. Yet her heart knew so much more.

Didn't it?

She turned her attention from Beth and Robert and slanted a gaze at Will. He watched the love-struck couple with a knowing grin on his face. Then he turned his head and caught her watching him. His grin deepened, revealing the twin clefts of his dimples, and spread into a smile. Her body pulsed in response and her heartbeat began a wild gallop. The man affected her, nothing to doubt there.

But what would become of them when they returned to their so very different lives? He would go back to his lovely townhouse in the West End, bantering with his sister and hobnobbing with aristocrats like Ashdowne, and Ada would return to The Golden Bell in the East End, with her overwrought mother, and the prospect of seeking new employment on the heels of a dismissal for immoral conduct.

After whispering to each other, Beth and Robert seemed resolved.

"I cannot come home with you just yet, Ada, but I will write a note for you to take back to Mother and share with Vicky."

Beth was a woman. The thought struck Ada, as if she had never allowed for the truth of it before. She was a woman and knew her own mind. Perhaps she knew her own heart too.

"Very well. Will you come in a fortnight?"

Beth turned her eyes toward Robert and some secret communication seemed to pass between them.

"Yes, a fortnight from today. Rob and I will meet you at Euston Station. We'll come on the early train."

The news that Mr. Cornforth would be accompanying her sister pleased Ada. It seemed the man opposite her at the small pub table would soon be a member of the family.

When they stood to make their farewells, Beth clung to Ada for a long while, much as she had as a young girl when a storm or nightmare frightened her. But when they pulled apart, Ada looked into the eyes of a wiser young woman. Wiser and apparently happier than she had ever been in London.

Ada and Will found a conveyance to take them to the station and were just in time for an early afternoon train. They settled into a first class carriage, much like the one they secured for their journey up to Derbyshire.

Will sat close, and Ada appreciated his nearness, the now familiar scent of him, and the warmth of his body. Desire coiled low in her belly, but her mind would not allow her to act. Doubts, dark and nagging, hung over her like the storm clouds chasing across the autumn sky.

It was easier to watch the landscape pass away through the windows of the train than face the man beside her. If she looked into those grey eyes, she wouldn't manage another sensible thought for the remainder of the journey.

He did not interrupt the silence between them, nor did he reach for her, as she half hoped he would. It seemed he would wait for her, and patiently, but he finally spoke, his voice low and calming.

"The countryside wears the autumn colors well."

It did. Every shade of orange and brown and red painted the trees, at least those that still clung to their leaves.

Ada felt her face crease in a grin. "Quite a change from Whitechapel."

"Will you miss it?"

"Derbyshire?"

Will smiled at her the way she smiled at Vicky when the child said something a bit silly but completely in earnest.

"I hope we will always have fond memories of Derbyshire, what little we saw of it. But I meant your home, Whitechapel. Will you miss it?"

A little flutter started in Ada's belly, not only of the desire she always felt for him, but of hope.

"How could I miss it? I live there."

"For now, yes, but I thought..." His grey eyes darkened as she watched him. The glimmer of pleasure that had been there the moment before was gone.

"Ada." He reached for her then, clasping her hand, and leaning closer, so close she could feel his voice reverberating in her chest. "Do you not know I wish to marry you?"

"Do you?" The flutter in her belly took flight, soaring up, spreading out, filling her with emotion too great to contain. Tears threatened to spill, but she swallowed hard, determined to hold them back.

"Well I did attempt to ask you, but you interrupted me. It's a very bad habit of yours, Miss Hamilton." His smile belied the jesting nature of his chastisement.

He rose from the bench seat beside her and struggled to arrange his long body on one knee before her. He leaned heavily on his cane as he bent. "This is when such a device becomes quite useful."

When he was before her, still clasping her hand, he opened his mouth as if to speak and then stopped, closing his mouth again.

"Have you changed your mind? I promise not to interrupt you this time," she urged.

He shook his head, his eyes never leaving hers.

"I have no ring to give you. You must have a ring."

She had never known frustration so acute, and Ada bit her lip to stop from crying out "Yes, yes, yes" before Will had even asked the question.

"Please." She did not know if it was proper to plead for a marriage proposal, but Ada was well past the point of behaving in the proper way.

"Will you, Miss Adaline—"

"How—"

"Ah!" He held up a finger. "That is interrupting. Matron Marley told me your name, if you must know. Should I continue?"

Ada nodded her head so vigorously she felt a hairpin come loose.

"Will you, Miss Adaline Hamilton, be my wife?"

She said the words—"Yes, yes, yes!"—that had been waiting to burst forth and nodded again and again—so many times that the hairpin finally fell, along with a thick strand of hair, and a steady stream of tears.

EPILOGUE

"ADA, DO YOU LIKE MY DRESS?"

Vicky stood in the Selsby's drawing room in front of Ada and spun around in a tight little circle, letting her new white gown with green flowers and trim fly out around her. The green satin ribbon Ada had saved for her from Will's box looked lovely woven through her dark locks.

"I adore it."

"Beth made the dress for me, and you gave me this ribbon. Do you remember?"

"I do, dearest."

Vicky looked Ada up and down from head to toe, a frown puckering her forehead.

"Aren't you going to wear something fine for Beth's visit?"

Ada looked down at her simple grey dress and wished she had something better. It was a well-cut dress, with flattering panels and pretty stitching around the cuffs, but it was past its prime and nothing like the height of fashion.

"I do not mean to interrupt, but I believe I have a solution." Kate stood in the doorway. A suspicious smile broadened her lips and, as usual, Ada found her soon-to-be sister-in-law difficult to decipher. "Come upstairs with me, Ada, and we'll soon sort you out."

Kate had a manner much like her brother's. Though her voice was resonant and pleasant, she possessed an air of command that made it difficult to refuse her anything.

Ada followed her up the stairs and into the sitting room where Kate often sewed and hosted luncheons with her ladies' society friends. Kate indicated a long settee covered with several boxes in various sizes.

"I forgot something. Let me just go and fetch him."

"Him?"

Ada approached and examined the boxes. Each was tied with a ribbon, two were green satin and one pure white.

"They are all for you."

Ada could not help the smile any more than she could the gooseflesh that pebbled her skin at the sound of his voice. She turned to look at him, but he was already behind her, wrapping his arms around her waist, pressing his body into hers, and nuzzling the stray strands of hair at her nape.

"Which shall I open first?"

"The middle one first."

Ada reached for the box between the others and slid its green ribbon aside. The lid popped off with a *whoosh* and white fabric frilled with delicate green lace slipped over the sides. It was a petticoat, the prettiest she'd ever seen.

"I promised I'd buy you another. Or twelve. I thought this would make a start."

Ada turned her head and Will kissed her cheek before moving his mouth to ear and whispering, urging her on.

"The big one next."

The largest box was heavy and so wide she inched one side of the lid up and then the other until it finally slid off. Emerald green satin filled the box. She saw stitches and ruchig and panels of lace, all in the same rich, vibrant shade.

Ada lifted the bodice, entranced by the silky slide of the fabric against her fingertips.

She looked back at Will.

"It's too grand."

"Nonsense. Now the last."

Ada reached for the smallest box, slipped aside its snowy satin ribbon, and lifted its lid to find a mystery within a mystery. Inside the main box were two smaller ones with wads of crumpled paper to cushion and keep them apart.

"That one first." Will pointed to the square box on the left.

This lid did not lift off but bent up on a hinge. Inside, on rich blue velvet, a ring glinted up at her in a rainbow of color. Small red faceted jewels surrounded a central fiery opal, all set on a gold band.

Too stunned to speak, Ada watched as Will lifted her hand in his and slipped the ring on her finger.

"I did say you needed a ring."

Ada was grateful for Will's strong body behind her, holding her up. She was lightheaded with joy, as if she might float away.

"There is one more."

"It's already too much."

And it was too much—too much happiness, too emotion bursting the seams of her heart, too much of the contentment she never dreamed she would find. And she did not wish it any other way.

She reached for the last box, a small rectangle, and found the rest of the broach's opals inside. They had been transformed into earrings, two teardrops of colorful white stone surrounded by smaller opal rounds.

When Ada said nothing, Will tensed behind her.

"Do you like them, love?"

She stroked his hand at her waist and turned her head to smile at him.

"I told you to give these opals to a woman who would cherish them, and you." Ada gazed at him, her eyes reflecting the emotions welling inside. "And you did."

He kissed her then, tenderly, lingering at her mouth for another kiss and another.

Ada was breathless when he pulled away and spoke to her, his tone earnest, as if proclaiming a solemn vow.

"We'll cherish each other."

ABOUT THE AUTHOR

Christy Carlyle writes sensual and sometimes downright steamy historical romance, usually set in the Victorian era or Regency period. She loves heroes who struggle against all odds and heroines that are ahead of their time. A former teacher with a degree in history, she finds there is nothing better than being able to combine her love of the past with her die-hard belief in happy endings.

To keep up with Christy's upcoming releases, read exclusive excerpts, and be the first to get notification of giveaways, sign up for her newsletter here.

You can also connect with Christy via Instagram or Facebook, or better yet, join her reader group, The Carlyle Club, on Facebook.

If you enjoyed this story, the kindest thing you can do for an author is to take the time to review his or her book on Amazon, Barnes & Noble, Kobo, Apple, or at Goodreads.

You can find Christy's Goodreads page at here.

Join my spam-free reader list and receive an introductory book, access to exclusive giveaways, and sneak peeks at new books.

Sign up here to get your free book.

ALSO BY CHRISTY CARLYLE

www.ingramcontent.com/pod-product-compliance
Lightning Source LLC
Chambersburg PA
CBHW061255170626
46809CB00007B/3001